Brock had wo~~rked~~
to know that yo~~u never~~ discounted
any threat.

From what Kate had told him about the call she'd taken at the Health Center, somebody sounded determined to cause problems. The fact that he'd ended the conversation with a promise to see Kate again concerned Brock most of all.

He had asked her earlier if she had any enemies on the island, and she'd said no. Now he wasn't so sure. Ean Thornton seemed to harbor anger against Kate for what he thought was an ongoing persecution of his son. Could Ean be the one wanting to harm Kate?

If someone was targeting her, Brock intended to help find out who it was. He would do everything in his power to see that she wasn't hurt. After all, he owed her that much.

Books by Sandra Robbins

Love Inspired Suspense

Final Warning
Mountain Peril
Yuletide Defender
Dangerous Reunion

SANDRA ROBBINS,

a former teacher and principal in the Tennessee public schools, is a full-time writer for the Christian market. She is married to her college sweetheart, and they have four children and five grandchildren. As a child, Sandra accepted Jesus as her Savior and has depended on Him to guide her throughout her life.

While working as a principal, Sandra came in contact with many individuals who were so burdened with problems that they found it difficult to function in their everyday lives. Her writing ministry grew out of the need for hope that she saw in the lives of those around her.

It is her prayer that God will use her words to plant seeds of hope in the lives of her readers. Her greatest desire is that many will come to know the peace she draws from her life verse, *Isaiah* 40:31—"But those who hope in the Lord will renew their strength. They will soar on wings like eagles, they will run and not grow weary, they will walk and not be faint."

DANGEROUS REUNION

SANDRA ROBBINS

Love Inspired

Recycling programs
for this product may
not exist in your area.

™ LOVE INSPIRED BOOKS

ISBN-13: 978-0-373-44451-9

DANGEROUS REUNION

www.LoveInspiredBooks.com

Printed in U.S.A.

And when ye stand praying, forgive, if ye have ought against any: that your Father also which is in heaven may forgive you your trespasses.
—*Mark* 11:25

ONE

Murder didn't happen on Ocracoke Island. But with a gun-shot wound in the center of Jake Morgan's back, Hyde County senior deputy Kate Michaels knew it had to be murder.

She glanced at Grady Teach, self-proclaimed island historian, who had discovered the body. "What were you doing at the beach so early this morning, Grady?"

Before he could answer, the police equipment bag she'd placed in the sand beside Jake's body exploded in a rush of air followed by the crack of a rifle. She pulled her service revolver from its holster and whirled to determine the shooter's position. The second shot kicked up sand inches from her feet.

Kate lunged for a stunned Grady and shoved him to the ground as another rifle report echoed across the quiet beach. The bullet sailed over their heads. "Stay down. Someone's shooting from the beach ridge dune," she screamed. She turned her mouth to her lapel mic. "Shots fired. Officer needs assistance at beach ramp."

"Ten-four." The reply crackled in the crisp morning air.

Another shot whizzed over their heads, and then silence.

A car engine roared and tires squealed on the pavement of the road that skirted the beach. Kate jumped to her feet and bolted across the two hundred feet of sand and up the hundred-foot-long wooden ramp toward the top of the dune ridge that ran parallel to the coastline. When she reached the road on the other side of the dunes, she looked in both directions, but the car had disappeared.

She ran toward the spot from where the shots had seemed to come—the overwash pass where storms had cut a low section into the dunes. She stared into the sea oats that covered the area. The tall, drooping clusters of seedheads had provided good cover for the shooter.

Kate squatted and parted the long stems to get a better look at the ground around their base. The shooter had also cleaned up after himself. There were no spent shells on the ground.

A siren wailed in the distance, and a squad car, its blue lights flashing, came into view from the direction of the village. Deputy Trainee Doug O'Neil, his gun in his hand, was out of the vehicle almost before it stopped. "What happened, Kate?"

"Somebody took some shots at us. Did you meet any cars on your way here?"

Doug shook his head. "No."

Kate stared in the opposite direction. "He must have gone that way. See if you can catch up to him."

The words were hardly out of her mouth before Doug was back in the car and speeding down the beach road. Kate watched until he disappeared into the distance before she slipped her gun back into its holster and headed down the ramp to the beach.

Grady still lay on the ground where she'd left him. He pushed to his feet as she approached. "I ain't never been so scared in my life, Kate. I thought we was dead for sure."

Kate had known Grady all her life and often laughed about his tendency to make everything that happened on Ocracoke his business. This morning she was sure he had gotten more involved than he'd wanted.

She reached out and gripped his shoulder. "Are you all right, Grady?"

He picked up his straw hat from where it had fallen in the sand and slapped it against his leg. He wiggled his finger between the matted gray hairs that hung over his ears and scratched his head before he deposited the hat back on his head. "Yeah, I'm all right. But I never thought finding Jake Morgan's body would almost get me killed."

Kate glanced back at the body and sighed. "I warned Jake he was going to end up like this. And we almost did, too."

She squatted beside the man lying facedown on the beach and shook her head. Jake Morgan—island bad boy, thief, drug dealer and a thorn in the flesh of law enforcement officers in three counties—had finally met someone who got the best of him. Even when she and Jake started first grade together in the old island schoolhouse, he was a troublemaker, challenging every boy in the school to a fight at one time or another. Regret for the wasted life of a childhood friend welled up in Kate, and she bit her lip.

"Okay, now where were we before the shooting began?"

Grady Teach shifted from one foot to the other. "Ain't you gonna call the sheriff about us almost gettin' killed?"

Kate shook her head. "I'll report this to Sheriff Baxter later, but right now he'd expect me to take care of the investigation. You know there are only three deputies assigned to this island, and one's off duty today. Doug's pursuing the shooter's vehicle. Maybe he'll find something. But whoever shot at us isn't going anywhere. There isn't another ferry off the island until noon. We'll stake out the line of boarding cars and see if we can find anything. Until then, I still have a murder here."

Grady's leathered skin wrinkled into a frown. "You're the law. I guess you know what you're doin'."

Kate sighed. "Now, tell me what happened this morning."

"Before the shooting started, I was just about to tell you that I seen him a-layin' here when I went for my mornin' walk."

"Did you touch anything, Grady?"

"Nope. I called you the minute I seen him. Knew there warn't nothing I could do to help him."

Kate pushed to her feet, propped her hands on her hips and glanced around. With the exception of the dead man at her feet and a shooter loose on the island, it looked like any other morning on the beach. It was still too early for the tourists to spread out across the sand for a day in the sun. The only person she could see was a jogger who approached from the south, his feet splashing a misty spray in the surf.

On the water the sun glinted on the white hull of a lone fishing skiff that cruised up the shoreline. It slowed and anchored about eight hundred feet offshore, its hull bobbing on the waves like the cork on a fishing line.

She turned and studied the jogger, who had come closer. A frown wrinkled her forehead, and she narrowed her eyes in order to get a better look. Something about him appeared familiar.

He reminded her of a movie she'd seen about athletes who trained by running on the beach. With his straight back, arms bent at the elbows and legs stretched in a lengthy stride, he could very well have been trained by her college track coach.

He drew closer, and his gait slowed. She opened her mouth to tell him to move on down the beach, but the words froze in her throat. Surprise flashed across his face as he stumbled to a stop a few feet away and stared at her. Her heart skipped a beat at the sudden revelation—he *had been* trained by her college track coach.

Kate glanced from the corpse to the runner. Two men she knew well. At her feet lay Jake Morgan, a guy who'd spent several years in prison for stealing. Facing her stood Brock Gentry, a thief of another kind. He'd once made her a victim by capturing her heart and trampling it in the process.

This couldn't be happening. Brock? After all these years, why was he here?

Brock, a surprised expression on his face, stopped a few feet away. "Hello, Kate. Is everything okay? I thought I heard shooting."

Kate opened her mouth to speak, but the words lodged in her throat. She swallowed and tried again. "Somebody took a shot at us. Did you see anybody down the beach?"

"No." He took a step closer. "Are you all right?"

"We're fine."

His gaze raked her from head to toe. A slight smile curled his lips as he took in her deputy's uniform. "You're a police officer here?"

Kate bristled at what she interpreted as cynicism in his voice. Before she could offer a retort, Grady laughed. "She's not just an officer. She's the chief deputy on the island."

Brock smiled. "Good for you, Kate. Just like your father."

She opened her mouth, but the words didn't want to come. "Wh-what are you doing here?" She clenched her fists at her sides and berated herself for stammering.

A frown flickered across his face. "I guess you could call it a vacation." He stared past her at the body. "Do you think your shooter had anything to do with your victim?"

"I don't know." She narrowed her eyes and stared at him. "You sound like a police officer."

His face flushed. "I'm a detective with the Nashville Police Department now."

Nashville, Tennessee? He'd traveled over eight hundred

miles to vacation on the North Carolina barrier island where they'd spent so much time together? Her instinct told her he had to have an ulterior motive for coming back, but she couldn't imagine what it might be.

She glanced back at Jake's body. This was insane. She was standing at a murder scene making small talk with the man who had broken her heart. She took a deep breath. "Good for you. That's what you always wanted."

He nodded and turned his attention back to the body. "Do you have much crime on Ocracoke?"

Kate pushed her sunglasses up on her nose and straightened to her full height. "No. Mostly drunk and disorderlies." She tilted her head to one side and struggled to regain her professional composure. "You're headed toward the village, so that must mean you ran past this spot earlier. Didn't you see the body then?"

He shook his head. "I jogged down the road coming out here. Then about a mile down the road I decided to run in the sand on the way back and detoured down onto the beach." He glanced up toward the road. "I guess I didn't look this way when I passed by."

"So you didn't see anything?"

"No. Sorry."

Kate took a deep breath. "That seems strange."

His eyes narrowed. "Not really. If I'd seen him, I probably would have thought he was a drunk sleeping it off on the beach." He took a step backward. "If you don't have any more questions, I'll go and let you get on with your work here."

Her fingers curled in her palms. "That's a good idea."

He turned and jogged away. He'd only gone a few yards when he called over his shoulder, "I'm going to be on the island for a few weeks. I'll come see you. We have a lot to catch up on."

A lot to catch up on? Brock Gentry was the last person on

earth she wanted to sit down with and relive old times. She was happy. She had her sisters to care for and an island full of residents and tourists to protect. She didn't need an ex-fiancé to remind her of another time in her life.

She watched him jog up the beach before she turned back to the body. A big grin covered Grady's mouth, and she frowned. "What?"

Grady shrugged. "He seemed like a nice feller."

A nice fellow? Kate supposed Brock appeared that way to most people, but she knew another side to him. How long had it been since she'd last seen him? Six years, but sometimes it seemed like yesterday.

It had been hard to get over him, but she'd done it. Lately weeks and sometimes months would pass that she hardly thought of him. The love she thought they'd shared had begun to fade from her memory, and for the first time she felt as if she could live again.

After all this time, he'd returned. But why? Knowing him as she did, he must have a good reason. It didn't matter why he'd returned. While he was here, she'd just have to make sure their paths didn't cross.

Although Brock wanted to glance back at Kate, he clenched his fists and willed himself to stare straight ahead as he jogged away. This wasn't how he'd planned to let Kate know he was on the island. He had wanted to call her and ask if he could come by her home and talk. Instead he had run into her at a murder scene.

He'd tried to act surprised that she was still on the island, but he was sure she didn't believe him. He knew she'd still be here. Ocracoke held a fascination for her, and she never could understand why it didn't for him. He wondered how many times he'd asked himself in the past six years what his life would have been like if he'd given in to Kate's wishes and agreed to live on Ocracoke after they were married.

At the time, all he'd wanted was a career in a large city police department, and he believed if she loved him she would support his choice. In the end, though, the lure of the island had won out, and she had stayed while he left to follow his dream.

Now he was back, and they had met again on the beach where they'd spent so much time arguing about their future six summers before. Meeting her at a murder scene had hardly been what he'd envisioned.

And she was chief deputy on Ocracoke. It appeared the island had a greater hold on her now, and she had moved on with her life. He rubbed the stubble on his chin. Too bad he hadn't learned how to do that.

He wondered what she would say when she found out he'd come to Ocracoke on a mission to find peace for his battered soul. When his life had fallen apart three months ago, the only thought that had saved his sanity was that he needed to talk to Kate, the one person who'd always understood him. But was he being selfish? After all this time, would she care about the problems in his life?

He had asked himself those questions and had come to the conclusion that whatever the cost, he had to try. He needed cleansing for his soul, and he wanted that elusive peace that hovered just out of his reach. He hoped he could find forgiveness here in the island paradise that she always said God created, but now Brock wasn't so sure. If there was a God, He had more important things to do than worry about somebody like him.

Kate watched as Doug walked down the ramp toward the murder scene and stopped beside her. He pulled off his hat and mopped at the perspiration on his forehead. "Sorry, Kate.

There wasn't a sign of anybody around. The shooter must have known the island well to have disappeared like he did."

Kate nodded. "Thanks for trying. We'll set up a watch before the ferry boards later."

Doug glanced down at the body. "What we got here?"

Kate pulled her thoughts away from the shooter and her disturbing thoughts about Brock Gentry and adjusted her sunglasses. "The first case of murder I can ever remember on Ocracoke."

Doug leaned over the corpse and studied it before he looked back at Kate. "I know him. He's the one who was in the fight I broke up in the parking lot over at the Blue Pelican Bar a few nights ago."

Kate nodded. "I saw your report on that incident. Who was the other person involved?"

"I can't remember his name right off. He was a tourist, and neither one of them wanted to talk about what they were fighting about. I suspected it might have been a drug deal gone bad, but I couldn't prove it. Neither one had drugs on them, and they didn't want to press charges. I let them go with a warning."

"Did you write down the other man's name?"

Doug nodded. "It's in the report. I'll check it out when we get back to headquarters."

Kate sighed. "Well, if he was a tourist, he could be gone by now. The ferries stay busy shuttling visitors back and forth to the mainland. But if Jake Morgan was dealing drugs like we've been trying to prove, his customers are going to have to look for another source."

Doug glanced at the body again. "Is there anything you need me to do?"

"We'll need to check all of Jake's hangouts and see if anybody remembers seeing him last night."

Doug nodded. "I'll get on that right away. Anything else?"

She pursed her lips and studied the body. "His clothes are wet. He must have been lying here at high tide." She turned to Grady. "What time was high tide last night?"

Grady cleared his throat and stepped closer. "Hoigh toide was at three o'clock this morning."

Doug's eyebrows arched. "Hoigh toide?"

Kate nodded. "People who've lived on Ocracoke all their lives have a special language, Doug. Sometimes the long *i* in a word becomes like the sound in *boy*. *Hoigh toide* is 'high tide.' So we know he died sometime around 3:00 a.m." She glanced at her watch. "I phoned Doc Hunter right after Grady called me about finding Jake. I thought he'd be here by now."

Doug pulled his cell phone from his pocket. "Do you want me to give him another call?"

She shook her head. "He was just finishing breakfast. Said he'd be here as soon as he pulled on some clothes. We'll give him some more time, but thanks, Doug."

Kate stuck her sunglasses in her shirt pocket and focused on the scene at her feet. Out of the corner of her eye, she could see the concentration on Doug's face. Fresh from college with a degree in criminal justice, he was eager to get some experience. He'd told her he thought he could learn a lot about working with people on the quiet island. She doubted, though, that he ever thought he'd be investigating a murder before breakfast on a warm summer day.

Grady stuck his hands in the pockets of the cutoff jeans he was wearing and inched forward. "Can I do anything to help?"

She shook her head. "No, but thanks. We'll just wait for Doc."

Kate turned, walked to the edge of the water and gazed out to sea. The fishing skiff she'd noticed earlier still sat anchored offshore. A slight breeze ruffled her hair, and she frowned at the chill that penetrated her body. It began at her feet, traveled up her legs and spread upward until the cold prickled her scalp.

She had never felt this sensation before, but she'd often heard her father, a career law enforcement officer, talk about the feeling he'd had several times at crime scenes. An icy inkling, he called it. He couldn't explain why it happened or where it came from, but he knew without a doubt that it served as a premonition that danger lurked nearby and things weren't always what they seemed. Was that what she was experiencing now?

Kate shaded her eyes with her hand and squinted in an effort to get a better view of the boat, but it was too far away. She looked over her shoulder at Doug. "Do you still have those binoculars in your cruiser?"

"Yeah. Do you need them?"

She nodded. "I'd like to check out that boat on the water."

Doug hurried to his car and was back in minutes with the binoculars. He handed them to her. "Why are you looking at that boat?"

"Just curious," Kate answered.

She held the binoculars to her eyes and stared across the waves toward the skiff. The figure of a man standing upright in the boat came into view. He wore a hooded sweatshirt and jeans. But it wasn't what he was wearing that made her heart skip a beat. It was the fact that he held a pair of binoculars to his eyes, and he appeared to be staring straight at the scene on the beach.

An irrational thought flashed into her head—she was being watched, studied like a specimen beneath the lens of a microscope. Almost as soon as the thought entered her head, she dismissed it. The man was a tourist, probably a fisherman who had stopped to see what was happening on the beach. She was overreacting because of the morning's events.

She started to turn away, but something drew her back to the boat. She put the binoculars to her eyes again. The man stared back at her. Who was he? Why was he out there, and why was he watching her? Could he have a connection to the murder or the shooter?

Doug inched closer to Kate. "What do you see?"

She pointed at the boat that hadn't moved. "There's a man looking at us."

He tilted his head to the side and frowned. "Aw, that's just some fisherman who's curious about what we're doing."

Kate glanced over her shoulder at Jake's still form in the sand and back at the skiff. The memory of bullets flying over her head sent a tingle down her spine. "I guess so. But it's the only boat around, and it's near a murder scene. When I saw it, I had this strange feeling that we were being watched." She handed Doug the binoculars. "I can't see anything on board that makes me think he's a fisherman. See what you think."

Doug put the binoculars to his eyes and scanned the small craft. After a moment, he handed the binoculars back to her. "I can't see any fishing rods or fish bags, but they could be lying flat on the deck. It's hard to tell from this distance what he has onboard, but it looks like he's leaving."

Kate reached for the binoculars and stared through them at the boat that moved slowly up the coastline. The lone man stood at the controls, his back to her. The hood still covered his head. She followed the boat's progress until it became a dot on the horizon.

Lowering the binoculars, she frowned and shook her head. What was the matter with her? Just because there had been a murder on the beach didn't mean she had to suspect every person she saw. The man in the boat was just a tourist who could have been stopped offshore for any number of reasons.

She had more important things to do than stand around wasting time. Taking a deep breath, she turned back to Jake Morgan's body.

He stood at the controls of the fishing skiff as he guided the boat along the coastline of Ocracoke. This really was a beautiful place—a nice place for families to vacation. Maybe that statement should be revised, he thought. Perhaps he should say that this island was a beautiful place at the present time. You never could tell what might happen in the future.

Take this morning, for instance. Nobody had expected to find a body on the white sands of a beach voted the most beautiful in the nation, but there it was. A dead man right where families with children would be playing later. What was that deputy thinking at the moment? Was she shocked at what she'd seen on the beach?

He glanced at the binoculars lying on the seat behind him and smiled. From his observations, she'd appeared to be efficient in her handling of the crime scene. If she thought that was something, wait until she saw what he had planned. She was about to face the biggest test of her career.

Opening the throttle, he tilted his head back and sang the opening line from one of his favorite songs, "The Winner Takes It All." That was what he intended to do—take it all.

TWO

Kate glanced at the clock on the squad car's dashboard as she pulled to a stop in front of the building that had housed the Ocracoke Police Station for the past thirty-five years. Ten o'clock. She didn't realize it had gotten so late.

Doc Hunter, who was also the island coroner, had taken longer than she expected to complete his assessment of Jake's body. In the end, though, he'd agreed with her that Jake had been murdered. She'd followed the ambulance that transported the body to the island health center, but her visit there had yielded no new leads. At this point, she could only hope the state lab in Raleigh could discover something during the autopsy—a requirement of all suspicious deaths.

Her phone conversation with Sheriff Baxter on the mainland had also delayed her getting back to the station. "You know I consider you second in command in our department, Kate, and I trust your judgment," he'd said. "I'm shorthanded on the mainland, and I need you to take care of this case. Just keep me posted on what's going on. Okay?"

He'd been relieved to turn the matter over to her, and she didn't mind. But she still had a flash of fear every time she remembered those bullets whizzing past her and Grady's heads.

She glanced in the rearview mirror and caught sight of

Doug pulling his car to a stop behind her. He stepped out and waved before he disappeared into the building. It didn't take much to figure out that Doug couldn't wait to see Lisa Wade, the dispatcher. He'd been smitten the first day he arrived on the island. Kate kept hoping that Doug would see how Lisa felt about Calvin Jamison, the third deputy on the island, but so far he didn't appear to have noticed.

Kate exited the car and stopped beside the curb to observe what she referred to as the Souvenir Shuffle. No matter what time of the day or evening during the summer months, tourists packed the streets of the only village on the island to search for that special something to take home from vacation.

Now with the sun climbing higher in the sky, the village had awakened, and tourists had emerged to begin their days. In their straw hats and tropical island T-shirts, they looked better suited for a beach in the South Pacific instead of a barrier island off the coast of North Carolina.

Families on bicycles crowded the narrow, two-lane road that twisted and turned through the village. Once the island had been discovered as a vacation destination, bicycles had become the choice of transportation. She'd given up keeping a count of all the bicycle rental places on the island.

A man jogged past, and the memory of Brock returned. Her stomach churned. She asked herself the question that had flashed in her mind over and over since their encounter: what was he doing on Ocracoke?

During their college years, he'd told her often that he didn't know how she'd stood growing up on such an isolated island twenty-five miles off the coast of North Carolina. He'd spent all his life in Raleigh, and he intended to live and work in a city.

She'd thought he would change his mind once he came to realize how peaceful life could be on the island, but she'd been wrong. He'd deserted her at a time when she needed him most.

Now he'd come back. But why? All she wanted was for him to stay as far away from her as possible. Something had died in her the day he boarded a ferry and left her behind to cope with the most frightening time of her life. She doubted if she'd ever trust anyone with her heart again.

Shaking her head to rid it of the troubling thoughts, she climbed the two front steps of the building and pushed into the station. The cool interior calmed her and felt good on her hot skin.

From her seated position behind the dispatch desk, Lisa Wade jumped to her feet and rushed to Kate. "Are you all right? I was scared to death when you called in that you were under fire."

Kate smiled. "I'm fine, Lisa."

Lisa studied her for a minute before she turned back to her desk. "You're having a rough morning."

If she only knew how hard it had really been. Kate rubbed her eyes. "Yeah. Any calls?"

"Doc Hunter called. He said the EMTs will leave on the four o'clock ferry with Jake's body. If you need anything else, let him know."

Kate was about to respond when Calvin Jamison walked in from the back room. "Calvin, what are you doing here?"

He held a cup of coffee toward her. "I just poured this for myself, but you probably need it more than I do. I went by the Sandwich Shop to get some breakfast, and I heard Grady talking about Jake. I thought you might need me. Besides, I don't have anything better to do."

Kate glanced at Lisa, who always seemed to glow when Calvin was around. And who could blame her? Calvin reminded Kate of one of the muscular men she saw on TV ads for the latest invention to sculpt your body into perfect shape.

He worked out every day, and it had paid off. With his dark complexion and black hair, some women on the island were glad to get a speeding ticket just so they could catch another glimpse of him when they came in to pay the fine.

"Thanks, Calvin. You can help Doug with patrol and the vehicle checkpoint for the noon ferry while I fill out the paperwork on the murder."

He nodded and walked toward the door. "Glad to. First I think you ladies deserve a morning treat. I'll go pick us all up something to eat on break." He stopped at Lisa's desk and smiled down at her. "I won't be gone long, Lisa. Do you want me to bring you a latte and a muffin from the Coffee Cup?"

Lisa's face beamed. "That would be nice, Calvin."

He glanced at Kate. "What about you?"

"Nothing for me, thanks."

Break time wasn't on her mind at the moment. She still hadn't shaken the feeling she'd had when she spotted that fishing skiff offshore. Then there was Brock Gentry. When she added a murder and a shooter to the mix, it was no wonder it was all running together in her head.

Calvin winked at Lisa and glanced around at Doug, who'd stood beside his desk across the room ever since Kate entered. "Ready to go, partner?"

Doug didn't answer. He picked up his hat and moved toward the front door. He didn't look at Kate or Lisa as he followed Calvin outside.

Lisa didn't glance at Doug as he walked by. Instead she directed her attention to her computer screen and bit her lip as if she was lost in another world.

Kate's heart pricked at the look on Lisa's face. Once she had been in love, too, but nothing good had come of that. She hoped Lisa would fare better than she had.

Kate walked into her office, dropped her sun visor on her desk and entered her private bathroom. She closed the door behind her, placed her hands on the small sink and peered into the mirror. Her tanned face stared back at her. She pressed her fingers to her cheeks and brushed the skin that was no longer as soft as it had been six years ago. Tiny creases at the corners of her tired eyes would be wrinkles before long. It was easy to see how the responsibilities and disappointments in life had taken a toll on her.

She wondered what Brock had thought when he saw her on the beach. What did she care what he thought? He meant nothing to her anymore, and she was sure he felt the same way.

Kate sighed and shook her head. With one last glance in the mirror, she pulled the door open and stepped into her office. She frowned at the sound of Calvin's voice and moved into the outer office. He stood at Lisa's desk.

"I thought you'd left."

Calvin's white teeth flashed behind his smile. "I forgot to ask Lisa if she wanted a blueberry or a banana muffin. But I'm leaving now."

Kate tried to suppress a grin. "It's nice to know you aim to please."

Calvin's face flushed, and he headed toward the door. He pulled it open and backed through it, but he stopped and turned to the person he'd bumped into. "Oh, sorry, sir. I didn't see you there. Come on in. Can we help you?"

He stepped aside, and Kate's heart plummeted to her stomach at the sight of Brock Gentry walking in the door. Brock smiled and stepped around Calvin. "Thanks." He glanced at Kate. "I need to see Deputy Michaels."

"She's right there." Calvin pointed to Kate, then waved to Lisa. "Be back in a minute with some muffins."

Kate stood frozen in place as Brock walked toward her.

"Are you Mr. Gentry?" Lisa asked.

"Yes."

Lisa glanced at Kate. "I didn't get a chance to tell you Mr. Gentry called a few minutes ago and asked if you were in."

He approached and stopped in front of her. "I hope this isn't a bad time, but I need to talk with you. Can you please spare me a few minutes?"

The soft-spoken words sent a warning through her. There was something different about Brock Gentry, and she searched his face for the answer. The self-confident swagger and the slightly arrogant attitude that had always been evident in his manner were gone. The old Brock would never have asked her permission for anything. He would have marched into her office and informed her he was there to speak with her. His blue eyes studied her for a reaction, and she wondered if he thought she might refuse to see him.

The smile he directed at her appeared sincere. If she were meeting him for the first time, she could imagine liking the man who stood before her.

She glanced at Lisa. "It's okay, Lisa. I know Mr. Gentry." She looked back at him and nodded toward her office. "Come on in."

Kate walked to her office, stepped inside and held the door for him to enter. She pointed to a chair in front of her desk. "Please have a seat." Closing the door, she took a deep breath before settling in her chair. She propped her elbows on top of her desk and laced her fingers. "What can I do for you?"

Brock studied her for a moment before he spoke. "How are you, Kate?"

That was a good question. At the moment she wasn't sure. She struggled not to betray her anger that he had returned to Ocracoke. "I'm fine."

He nodded. "Good." He leaned back, gripped the arms of his chair and let his gaze drift around the office. "I remember sitting in this room and talking with your father. Now you occupy his place here. I ran into our old track coach a few months ago, and he told me your father had died. I was sorry to hear that."

Kate reached for a stack of papers on her desk and began to straighten them. "Yes, three years ago."

She glanced at him, and his eyes flickered with sadness. "I sent your father a few emails after we ended our engagement, but he never answered. I guess he blamed me for what happened, but I'm really sorry I didn't know about his death."

Kate shoved the papers aside and clasped her hand to keep from striking her desk top. "Would you have sent condolences? I don't remember you sending any when my mother died."

He shook his head. "No, I didn't, but there were reasons for that."

Her heart pounded in her chest, and she feared that he could hear it. "And what would they have been?"

He raked his hand through his hair. "Come on, Kate. We'd just had a bad breakup. I knew how you must be grieving over your mother's death, and I didn't want to cause you any more pain. But I have a standing order at the Baskets and Blooms to place flowers on your mother's grave each year on her birthday."

Kate's eyes widened, and she gasped. The arrival of the bouquets delivered to the cemetery had been a mystery for years. The owners at the flower shop had informed her they didn't know the identity of the buyer and that payment always came from a mainland law office that wouldn't reveal their client's name. She would never have dreamed they were from Brock. "Those are from you? But why?"

He shrugged. "It's a way I can show how I felt about a remarkable woman."

A memory flashed into her mind. The day Brock left the island he had taken her mother to the beach, and they had been gone a long time. When they returned, Kate met him coming out of the guest room with his suitcase in his hand. He'd pushed past her and walked out the door. That was the last time she had seen him until today.

Kate took a deep breath. "I—I don't know what to say but thank you."

Brock smiled. "There's no need to thank me." He shifted in his chair and leaned forward, his arms resting on his thighs. "But that's not why I'm here. I know you're busy, and this may not be a good time for me to drop by. But when I saw you on the beach earlier, I knew the sooner I came to see you the better off I'd be."

Kate frowned. "I don't understand. If you thought I'd order you off the island when I saw you, you don't have to worry. As long as you don't break any laws while you're here, our paths probably won't even cross."

"I know that. But the thing is, I want our paths to cross. I came back to Ocracoke to see you, Kate. I need your help."

The heartbreak of six years ago boiled up inside of her. *He* needed *her* help? Where was he when *she* needed *him?* She narrowed her eyes. "How could you ask me for anything?"

He swallowed, and his Adam's apple bobbed. "I know it shocks you, and I wouldn't blame you if you asked me to leave. This is the hardest thing I've ever had to do. Just please hear me out before you make a decision."

She picked up a pencil on her desk and rolled it between her fingers. "Very well. What do you want to tell me?"

He took a deep breath. "Let me start by saying that three months ago I wouldn't have believed I would ever come back here. I knew how you felt about me, and I don't blame you for that. But I've had something happen in my life that has nearly driven me over the edge. I've been going to counseling, but nothing has helped."

The fact that Brock had even used the word *counseling*,

much less been involved in it, shocked Kate. "You've been to counseling? You used to say that counseling was for the weak. That people who were in control of their lives didn't need some high-paid shrink to sit and have a pity party with them."

He nodded. "Yeah, that's what the old Brock said, but things changed. A few months ago something happened, and my life collapsed around me."

Kate frowned and leaned forward. "What?"

Brock bit his lip and thought for a moment before he spoke. "When I joined the police force in Nashville, I heard about a ten-year-old murder case. A local man named Robert Sterling was accused of killing his business partner. He was found guilty and sentenced to death. His attorneys had appealed the case for years, but they hadn't been able to get a new trial."

"Did you know the man?"

Brock shook his head. "No, but I'd read about the case, and I knew he was on death row. Anyway, late one afternoon I was alone in the office when my phone rang. It was a man who said that he'd wrestled with his conscience for years and that he could prove Robert Sterling was innocent. He said he was facing some serious surgery and that he didn't want to die without telling what he knew."

"Did you believe him?"

"I didn't know. I told him we were interested in what he had to say. Since he was so sick, I told him my partner and I would come see him the next day. He agreed. I took his name and phone number and told him I'd call him the next morning to arrange a time. I also told him we would check out anything he told us. He said it was crucial that we get on this right away because Sterling's execution date was only a few weeks away."

Kate exhaled. "It sounds like he was sure the man was innocent."

Brock nodded. "I thought so, too. I hung up and was getting ready to leave for the day when the phone rang again. It was a friend of my father's in Los Angeles. He was calling to tell me that Dad had been in a serious car accident and wasn't expected to live. He was asking to see me before he died."

Kate's eyes grew wide. "Your father? I didn't think you had any contact with him."

"I hadn't in years, not since he deserted my mother and me when I was ten years old. I knew if my father was calling for me, I had to see him and ask him why he never got in touch with me when I was growing up." Brock's eyes filled with tears, and his lips quivered. "Do you understand how important that was to me?"

"Yes, Brock. I understand."

He took a deep breath. "I scribbled a note to my partner and asked him to follow up on the Robert Sterling matter the next morning. Then I left it on his desk and rushed home. Within hours I was on a plane to Los Angeles." He hesitated for a moment. "The good news is that my father didn't die. I ended up staying with him for six weeks, and they were some of the happiest of my life. We bonded for the first time, and all of a sudden I had the father I'd always wanted."

Kate smiled. "I'm glad, Brock. I remember how you always wanted to know him."

His face clouded. "But there's more. The bad news is that when I returned home, I discovered my partner had never found the note I left for him. He didn't read it, he didn't contact the witness and Robert Sterling was executed."

Kate gasped and clamped her hand over her mouth. She stared at Brock and lowered her hand. "How horrible."

"It is, but there's more. When I failed to call the witness, he tried to reach me. Whoever he talked to at the station evidently didn't know I'd left town. They put him through to my voice mail to leave a message."

"And no one checked your messages?"

Brock shook his head. "No. The man entered the hospital the next day and had his surgery. He was sedated for days. When he was finally conscious, he realized nothing had been done. That's when he called Sterling's lawyers. They went to the district attorney but were unable to get the case reopened, and Sterling was executed. The lawyers broke the story to the newspapers along with my name."

Kate couldn't believe what she was hearing. As a police officer, she knew how devastating it could be if a miscarriage of justice caused an innocent person to suffer, let alone be killed. She wanted to go around the desk and comfort Brock, but she remained in her seat. "I'm so sorry, Brock."

"Yeah, me, too. I was cleared by my superiors of any wrongdoing, but I can't forgive myself, Kate. I keep asking myself why I didn't ask the chief when I called to update him on my father's condition if they'd questioned the witness. The only answer I have is that I was so worried about my father, I wasn't thinking about anything else." He paused and took a deep breath. "And now there's a law professor and a group of his students who are digging into Sterling's case. It looks like he was innocent after all."

"Have you talked to the witness since you came back from California?"

Brock shook his head. "No. He died while he was still in the hospital. The doctors said it was a heart attack."

Kate frowned. "This sounds like it was a series of mishaps that no one could have prevented. You can't blame yourself for what happened."

Brock stared at her with tortured eyes. "But I do, Kate. I should have followed through on what the man told me."

Kate took a deep breath. "You can't change what's happened. You're going to have to find a way of living with it."

He leaned back in his chair. The muscle in his jaw twitched. "That's why I'm here."

She sensed he was about to tell her something she'd rather not hear. "I don't understand."

His elbows rested on his knees, and he leaned forward. "I didn't come here to dredge up old memories, Kate, but there's one that's haunted me for years. I haven't been able to get it out of my mind for the past three months."

She didn't want to hear what haunted him. She had her own memories to deal with. She needed to tell him to go, to leave before he reopened wounds she'd thought healed. She started to rise. "I don't think it will do any good to relive the past, Brock."

He held up his hand to stop her. "Please. Hear me out."

She didn't want to hear him out. She wanted him to go, but the pleading look he directed at her begged her to listen. She nodded. "All right."

"When we graduated from college six years ago, we each went home for the summer. But I came to Ocracoke in June for us to plan our fall wedding. Remember?"

Kate struggled to show no emotion on her face, but her heart pounded in her chest. "I remember."

"I knew your mother was dying of cancer, and I wanted to help you get through the ordeal of losing her. As heartbroken as I was over that, I wasn't prepared that you'd decided you had to stay on Ocracoke after her death and take care of your family."

The corners of Kate's mouth puckered into tight lines. "Are you forgetting that I had two sisters who were sixteen and four years old who were about to lose their mother? Not to mention a father who was devastated. They needed me." She spat the words at him.

He didn't flinch from the anger in her voice. "I know, but you made your decision without discussing it with me. You had assumed I would agree and live with you here. When I told you I didn't want that, we decided it was best if we call off the wedding."

"If I remember correctly, you decided to call off the wedding. I thought you'd find a job on the mainland and commute so that I could stay here and take care of my two younger sisters."

Brock raked his hand through his hair. "I told you how unreasonable that was. It's a two and a half hour ferry ride to the mainland from here, and then it's another fifty or sixty miles to a town with a large police force. I didn't want that kind of commute every day. I thought you'd understand that."

Kate started to rise from her chair again. "I don't want to discuss our history, Brock. Maybe you should leave."

"No." He jumped up and planted his palms on her desk. "Please let me finish."

She hesitated a moment before she sank down in the chair. "Okay, but make it fast."

He nodded and eased back into his chair. "I will. Whatever happened then is in the past, but I have to tell you one more thing that happened that summer. On the last day I was here, your mother felt better, and she asked me to take her out to the beach. She wanted to watch the waves roll in. We sat on the sand, and she told me about her life on the island, how much she loved her family and about her peace of dying. She said she'd trusted God all her life, and now she was ready to trust him after death."

Tears burned Kate's eyes. "That sounds like her."

Brock clenched his hands in his lap and stared down at them. When he looked up again, Kate saw a hint of tears in his eyes. "Then she said she was sorry that her dying had caused you and me to break up. I tried to convince her she wasn't at fault, but she just smiled that sad little smile that said she knew better. She stared at the waves for a long time.

Then she said she knew how much I'd missed having a father, but there was another father who wanted to love me and show me the special plan He had for my life."

Kate closed her eyes, and she imagined how her mother must have looked that day. She could almost hear her mother's soft voice speaking of God's love as she did so often. "What did you say?"

"You know I never put much stock in the existence of God, but I didn't want to upset her. I thanked her for her concern. Then she turned to me and said, 'We can't go through life without God. Someday you're going to think your life is falling apart. Think of me sitting on this beautiful beach God created and come back to Ocracoke. God is everywhere here, Brock. All you have to do is look for Him, and you'll find the peace you need.'"

Kate sat in stunned silence before she was able to speak. "Did she say anything else?"

He shook his head. "No, but like I said, I can't get her words out of my mind. Maybe she realized that with the attitude I had that it was only a matter of time before something would knock me down, and she wanted me to know where I could find help."

Kate blinked back tears. "Did you come back thinking I'd help you?"

He stared into her eyes. "I suppose I hoped so, but I didn't dare let myself believe you would care what happened to me one way or another. I don't want to cause you any problems, Kate, but I've come to the point in my life that I need the peace your mother talked about. I figured the first step would be trying to gain your forgiveness."

Kate pushed to her feet and walked to the window. With her back to Brock she stared out at the alley that ran behind the building. Mixed emotions surged through her—happiness for Brock's reconciliation with his father, sorrow for the death of an innocent man and leftover anger from years ago. Now he wanted her forgiveness.

She whirled around to unleash her rage on him, but the sight of him slumped in the chair touched her heart. How could she disregard the words of hope her mother had given to Brock? Then there were the flowers for her mother's grave. She walked over to where Brock sat and stopped beside him. "After all that's happened between us, it must have taken a great deal of courage to come here."

She steeled herself for the old Brock to give a flippant answer. When he spoke, she knew the words came from his heart. He took a deep breath. "It did, but I meant what I said, Kate. Please believe me."

She reached out to touch his shoulder but drew her hand back before it made contact. "My mother was the most forgiving person I've ever known, and she tried to teach her children that trait. Although I know Jesus expects us to follow the example He gave us, I'm afraid I haven't reached that point yet. I can't promise I will ever forgive you, but I will promise that I'll pray about it. In the meantime you have to find your own way to God. He's there waiting. Maybe you're not listening."

He nodded and pushed to his feet. "That could be true. I know hearing me out hasn't been easy for you because you probably still hate me. But maybe we can heal some old wounds while I'm on the island." He held out his hand. "Can we try to be friends again?"

Kate stared at his hand for a moment. "I don't—"

"I'm not asking to go back to where we were. Just friends. I think your mother would want us to be." He arched his eyebrows and after a moment she slipped her hand into his. He grasped it and squeezed. "Thank you, Kate. Maybe we can start off by meeting for lunch today."

She shook her head and pointed to her waiting paperwork. "I can't, Brock. I'm too busy. Maybe some other time."

"You have to eat. Just lunch. That's all."

What would one lunch hurt? She sighed and pinned him with her gaze. "I take my lunch break at one o'clock. I can't promise, but I'll try to be at the Sandwich Shop then. That's the best I can do."

He smiled and backed toward the door. "I'll be waiting in case you can make it."

Kate heard him tell Lisa goodbye as he walked through the outer office, and then the door closed. She dropped into her chair and clasped her hands on her desk. What had she done?

Some days she didn't think about Brock at all, and she'd considered it a good sign that she had finally dismissed him from her life. Now he'd shown up with a story that had ripped her heart. Her mother had always felt God's presence on the beaches of Ocracoke as she watched the waves roll in. Kate could imagine how she must have looked the day she talked with Brock.

Now Brock had come back because of words spoken by her mother six years ago. She'd always known her mother had a special insight into the needs of others. Even when she was dying, she'd wanted Brock to know the joy she'd had from living her life for the God she loved.

Her mother had taught her that Jesus never turned away someone who was hurting, and a true believer would never do that, either. Maybe in some way her mother had known that after her death Kate would shoulder overwhelming responsibilities. And she had. Her mother had also known how hurt Kate was over the broken engagement and how hard it was for her to forgive. Perhaps her mother had been thinking of her, also, at the time.

If so, then this could be God's way of helping her, too. In

searching for Brock's peace of mind, she might also learn to forgive and put all the hurts of the past six years behind her.

If she could do that, being around Brock Gentry would be worth it in the long run.

THREE

Brock leaned against the railing around the deck of the Sandwich Shop and scanned the traffic on the street below. How many minutes past one was it now? He fought the urge to check his watch again. It couldn't have been more than a minute since the last time he'd looked. He'd give her some more time. After all, she had to deal with that murder and couldn't drop everything to rush off to lunch.

What if she ignored his invitation? He pushed away from the railing, turned his back to the street and strode to the far end of the deck. Doubts drifted into his mind. Perhaps he shouldn't have come to Ocracoke. It might be too soon to expect her to sit down for a meal with him. He should have waited before he spilled the story about Robert Sterling's death and that last day he spent with Kate's mother.

He straightened his shoulders and took a deep breath. She wasn't coming today. There was nothing for him to do but go back to the bed-and-breakfast where he was staying.

He whirled to leave, but his breath caught in his throat at the sight of Kate climbing the steps from the street to the deck. Even in uniform with a gun, handcuffs, magazine holder and assorted equipment hanging from her duty belt, she was more beautiful than he remembered. Her chestnut hair, parted in the middle and slicked back into a bun in police academy style, gleamed in the sun. Her willowy body and the slight sway of her hips when she walked reminded him of a runway model. Her dark brown eyes only added to the fascination that had overcome him the first time they met.

A frown puckered her forehead as she approached, but it disappeared when she stopped in front of him. "I'm sorry I'm late, but I got tied up over at the ferry with the other deputies. We were checking the cars leaving the island."

He nodded. "Were you hoping to find the shooter from this morning?"

"We thought we might get lucky, but all we found were vacationing families who were heading for home. Maybe I was expecting to see something suspicious, but I didn't. That may mean our shooter is still on the island. He could be a local who knows his way around. If he is, then he could be in plain sight all the time, and I wouldn't know it."

He tried to concentrate on her words, but his relief that she had come made it difficult. He smiled what he hoped was a friendly gesture. "You'll find him, Kate. But you must be starved after the morning you've had. Let's get something to eat."

She glanced at her watch. "I don't have much time."

Brock pointed to a table near the back of the deck. "Why don't we sit back there? I'll go inside and order. Do you need a menu, or do you know what you want?"

Kate chuckled. "I think I know everything they serve here. I'll have the Cajun pork sandwich and a glass of iced tea."

Brock nodded. "I'll be right back."

Ten minutes later he juggled a tray loaded with two sandwiches, two glasses of iced tea and a basket heaped with French fries. She picked up one of the teas without speaking and took a long drink. "It's been a long morning. I didn't realize how thirsty I was."

They ate in silence for a few minutes. Out of the corner of

his eye Brock watched the people entering and leaving the Sandwich Shop. A man and woman exited with a little boy about five years old. The woman leaned down to hear something the child was saying and burst out laughing. Turning to the man, she said something to him. He laughed, scooped up the little boy and set him on his shoulders. The three walked down the stairs to the street and within seconds were lost in the crowd.

He'd witnessed scenes of happy families together before, but today it affected him differently than before. The love the three shared showed on their faces. What would life be like if he and Kate had married? The truth was that no woman had looked at him that way since Kate, and it made him sad.

"Is something wrong?"

Kate's voice penetrated his thoughts, and his body stiffened. Glancing down, he realized he'd been holding his sandwich in front of his mouth the whole time he was watching the family. His face warmed, and he laid his food down and smiled.

"I was just thinking how good it is to see you again." He picked up his glass of tea and held it in front of him. "Here's to old friends."

She only hesitated a moment before she picked up her glass and clicked it against his. "To old friends."

He chugged a drink of iced tea and relished the cold sensation sliding down his throat. Kate set her glass down, and the smile she directed at him set his heart to thudding. Suddenly he realized how much he had missed her, but it didn't matter. The events he'd set in motion six years ago couldn't be changed any more than he could bring Robert Sterling back to life.

Now he'd returned begging for Kate's help. He had dreaded telling her why he'd come to the island, and now that he had, he wondered what she thought. The one thing he hadn't told her, though, was that when his life had fallen apart three months ago, he had come to the conclusion that he was being punished for the selfish choices he'd made in the past.

That and his guilt over Robert Sterling's death had brought him back to Ocracoke. He'd come for three reasons—to search for that elusive peace Kate's mother told him about, to cleanse his soul for failing an innocent man and to gain her forgiveness.

He'd told her he wanted to find God here in the island paradise she said He created, but now Brock wasn't so sure he could. One of the Ten Commandments his mother used to say to him was *Thou shalt not kill*. To his way of thinking he had helped kill Robert Sterling.

He doubted if there was any absolution for that sin.

He lowered the copy of the island newspaper just enough to stare over the top at the couple sitting at the table across the Sandwich Shop deck. He stared at Kate a moment before he glanced back at the front-page picture of her beside the article about island safety. *What an appropriate subject,* he thought.

The picture didn't do her justice, though. She was much more attractive in person, and she appeared to be more relaxed than she'd been earlier this morning when he observed her through the binoculars. But she'd been at a murder scene then, and she'd probably been worried about having a killer on the island that the newspaper touted as the safest on the eastern seaboard.

However, there were many dangers on a remote island, and it was impossible to determine when one might strike. In a split second some unforeseen tragedy could occur that would shatter the tranquil image of a vacation paradise that the publicists up and down the barrier island chain worked to promote.

He closed his eyes and inhaled deeply. Too bad no one else could sense what he knew was about to come. When he was finished, this island and Kate and her friend would never be the same again. He would make sure of that.

In fact, the fun should start any minute now. He glanced at his watch.

A loud boom shattered the afternoon stillness.

Kate sprang from her chair and scanned the area in an effort to see where the sound had come from. Other customers on the deck of the Sandwich Shop bounded to their feet, but everyone appeared frozen in stunned silence.

Kate's lapel mic crackled. "Ten-eighty in alley next to the Sun Shop. Possible injury."

"Ten-four. Get the EMS en route," Kate replied.

Kate ran across the deck with Brock right behind. He called out to her. "Did I hear your dispatcher say a bomb had exploded?"

"Yes."

At the bottom of the steps she turned right and raced down the street toward the Sun Shop. As she approached, customers poured out the front door and streamed down the steps of the store that boasted the lowest-priced T-shirts on the island. Kate rounded the corner of the building and into the alley. A teenage boy lay on the ground halfway down the narrow pathway.

"Stay back! Let Deputy Michaels take care of this situation." Behind her Brock's voice of authority barked out the order, and she turned to see him blocking the entrance to the alley.

The teenager on the ground struggled to sit up. Kate's hand on his shoulder restrained him. "Don't move. There's an ambulance on the way."

The boy's face paled as he caught sight of the blood pouring from his leg. He sank back on the ground and groaned. Kate knelt beside him. "I'm going to look at your injury."

The teen wore mesh athletic shorts that came to his knees. Blood poured from a gaping hole halfway down his shin. The wound needed a tourniquet right away.

Kate unhooked her duty belt and placed it on the ground. With a quick tug she yanked the belt in the pants loops of her uniform free and wrapped it around the boy's leg just above the wound. He groaned as she pulled it as tight as she could. "You're going to be all right. Try to lie still. The ambulance will be here any minute."

It seemed an eternity before she heard the familiar wail. Brock's voice rose above the ambulance's siren. "All right, folks. You need to move so the ambulance can back into the alley. Please get out of the way."

Kate looked over her shoulder as the Ocracoke Emergency Vehicle backed toward her. Before the driver had stopped, one of the EMTs jumped from the passenger side and ran to the teen on the ground.

He dropped to his knees next to Kate. "Thanks, Kate. I'll take over now." He studied the wound and glanced back up at Kate. "What caused this?"

Kate grabbed her duty belt from the ground and pushed to her feet. "It was an explosion. I don't know what yet."

She replaced the equipment around her waist as the second EMT rushed past her and knelt next to the boy who seemed alert. The man squeezed the teenager's shoulder and smiled. "That's a nasty wound you got there. What happened?"

He shook his head. "I don't know. I cut down this alley to get to the house my family rented on the next street. I saw this two-liter soda bottle on the ground. Just before I got to it, the thing blew up."

Kate glanced around the alley. Pieces of a plastic bottle littered the area. At that moment Doug and Calvin pushed through the crowd and stopped next to her. Calvin glanced at the boy and back at her. "What happened?"

"Somebody left a bottle bomb in the alley. This kid happened by just as it exploded."

Calvin shook his head. "Who would leave something like that?"

Brock walked over to them and stopped beside Kate. "I've seen a lot of these in Nashville. This boy is lucky he wasn't hurt worse."

Calvin frowned and glanced from Brock to Kate. "Didn't I see you earlier at the station?"

Brock nodded. "I'm Brock Gentry. I was with Kate when the bottle exploded."

Kate's face warmed under the surprised gazes on Calvin's and Doug's faces. "Brock is a policeman in Nashville. We knew each other in college."

Calvin stuck out his hand. "Welcome to Ocracoke, Brock. I hope you don't think we always welcome tourists this way."

He cocked an eyebrow and grasped Calvin's hand, then Doug's. "Glad to meet two fellow officers."

Calvin and Doug turned questioning glances toward Kate, and her face grew warm. She pointed to the bottle fragments. "Calvin, you and Doug gather up all the remains you can find. I'm going to the Health Center with this boy. After Doc checks him out, he may be able to remember something that will help us catch whoever left this thing." Kate watched them walk away before she turned back to Brock. "I guess our lunch is over. It's back to work for me."

He smiled. "I understand. I'll go back to where I'm staying for now." He hesitated before he turned. "Can I see you later?"

She shrugged. "I don't know what this afternoon will bring, and my sisters and I are having dinner with Treasury Wilkes. She's been like a second mother to us since our parents died."

He smiled. "Then that's perfect. I'm staying at Ms. Wilkes' bed-and-breakfast, and she invited me to dinner tonight."

Kate's mouth gaped. "You're staying at the Island Connection Bed-and-Breakfast?"

"Yes. I remembered her from when I was here before. So that was where I wanted to stay."

"It's a second home to my sisters and me."

He turned away from her, placed his hand on the back of his neck and rubbed. When he faced her again, he sighed. "I remember Mrs. Wilkes was your mother's best friend. If it makes you uncomfortable for me to stay there, I'll move somewhere else."

She shook her head. "Of course you can stay there. After all, it's the best bed-and-breakfast on the island."

A smile flashed across his face. "Good. Then I'll see you there."

Before she could respond, he turned and walked from the alley. When he disappeared, she glanced back at Calvin and Doug, who appeared engrossed in their task of collecting evidence and placing it in the plastic bags they held.

They had never experienced a day like this on Ocracoke. First a murder, shots fired at an officer and an island resident, and now a victim of an exploding bottle. With hundreds of tourists arriving and departing each day, finding out who left the bottle in the alley, who killed Jake or who tried to kill her promised to be a daunting task. That didn't matter, though. As long as she was an officer of the law, she would do everything in her power to protect the citizens and tourists on Ocracoke. The one thing she did dread, however, was that she had agreed to help the one person in the world she'd hoped she would never see again.

Summer had just started, and it already threatened to be like no other. Shaking her head, she headed to her squad car.

Thirty minutes later after a stop by the police station, Kate stepped into the Health Center and looked around the deserted waiting room. No one sat at the reception desk.

She started to call out for Sharon, the receptionist, but she stopped when the telephone on Sharon's desk rang. Kate waited for a moment before she stepped to the door and peered down the hall that was lined with examining rooms. "Doc, your phone's ringing."

"That you, Kate? Sharon's at lunch. Will you see who's calling?"

Kate had learned long ago that a police officer's duties on Ocracoke required more than keeping the peace. It also meant serving the needs of the residents, and right now Doc needed someone to answer the phone. Smiling, she plopped down in the chair behind Sharon's desk, cleared her throat and picked up the receiver. "Ocracoke Health Center. May I help you?"

"I'm trying to reach Deputy Michaels. I saw her enter the Health Center a few minutes ago."

Kate's skin prickled at the singsong voice on the phone, and she tightened her grip on the receiver. "This is Deputy Michaels. How can I help you?"

"I wanted to check on that poor boy who was hurt at the Sun Shop."

"Are you a family member?"

A low chuckle sounded. "Oh, no."

Kate reached for a pencil. "I'm sorry. I didn't catch your name."

"That's because I didn't give it."

Kate's heart pounded. She didn't know who this was, but something told her he was up to no good. "I'll ask you again. How can I help you?"

He laughed. "I really caused an uproar with my bomb, didn't I? It was quite exciting to watch."

Kate sat up straight in the chair and gripped the receiver tighter. "You left that bottle bomb? But why?"

"It's not time for you to know the answer to that, but you will soon."

Kate gritted her teeth. "Look, whoever you are, don't you realize that boy could have been killed?"

"I know, but he wasn't. He didn't look dead to me when they loaded him into the ambulance."

Anger boiled up in Kate. "Wanting to hurt someone you don't even know sounds sick."

"I assure you I'm not sick." His voice hardened with each word.

A thought popped into Kate's head. "You wouldn't happen to be wearing a hooded sweatshirt and jeans, would you?"

He chuckled. "Very good, Deputy Michaels. You've caught on to me. I must confess I was wearing those items when I saw you at the beach."

The icy inkling she'd had earlier flowed through her body. "So you were watching from that fishing skiff. Why? Did you kill Jake?"

"Jake?" The voice held a hint of surprise. "Oh, you mean the man on the beach. Well, you're the police expert. I'm sure you'll figure it out sooner or later. But I must say, I thought you handled that crime scene quite well. I enjoyed watching you."

"And did you arrange for the shooter?"

"My, my, Deputy. You're just full of questions, aren't you?"

Kate's fingers tightened on the receiver. "That's part of my job. I ask questions so I can find people who break the law." She paused for a moment and took a deep breath. "Your voice is unfamiliar to me, so I know you don't live on Ocracoke.

Why would you come to a place where families are vacationing and try to hurt someone?"

Laughter rumbled in her ear. "I'm not interested in the tourists, Deputy Michaels. It's you who fascinates me. Before long, you'll be wishing I'd gone somewhere else besides Ocracoke. There's the title of an old song that I want you to think about over the next few days. It's one especially for you, Kate."

"What song?"

"'I'll Be Seeing You.'"

The whispered words drifted into her ear as if they rode on a foggy mist. They flowed through her body, giving her a sense of helplessness and vulnerability like she'd never experienced. Her heart pounded, and the cold sensation she'd felt on the beach earlier coursed through her veins. Someone she didn't know was watching her movements and had spoken the most chilling words she'd ever heard.

Kate opened her mouth to speak, but the phone line went dead. Kate pulled the receiver from her ear and stared at it. She punched the caller ID button and shook her head when *Private number* was displayed.

Placing the phone back in its cradle, she replayed the phone conversation and what she'd learned from it in her head. She now knew she was right about someone watching from the fishing skiff earlier this morning. He had also admitted leaving the bottle bomb. He hadn't admitted to killing Jake or arranging for the shooter, and that puzzled her. Why wouldn't he take credit for those as well? And most of all, why was he fascinated with her?

She stood, walked to the window and looked up and down the street. She saw no parked cars or anyone walking on the sidewalk. Yet the caller said he'd seen her at the Sun Shop and as she entered the Health Center. Chills raced up her spine at the thought of how his voice sounded. The menacing whine of impending danger rang through her mind.

She didn't know what was about to happen, but she did know one thing: someone with an unknown agenda walked around Ocracoke, and he'd made her his target. Maybe Jake had been his first. She prayed that she could find this mysterious person before he carried through with his intentions.

Kate stepped back from the window and closed her eyes for a moment. She had no idea who he was or where she should begin looking for him—but when she found him, she would come face to face with pure evil.

FOUR

Late that afternoon Kate pulled her squad car to a stop in the driveway behind the Island Connection Bed-and-Breakfast. She switched off the ignition and rubbed her eyes. She didn't know when she'd ever been so tired. The thought of a relaxing bath and a good night's sleep tempted her to crank the car again and head for home, but she had promised Treasury she would come for dinner.

She lay against the headrest for a moment and closed her eyes. Dinner tonight could prove to be uncomfortable. She climbed from the car and had taken only two steps toward the back porch when a gray ball of fur swept past her feet. Startled, she jumped backward and stared at her little sister's cat dashing across the backyard.

"Rascal," she muttered. Sometimes she thought the six-toed Maltese cat took great pleasure in scaring the wits out of her.

She watched Rascal disappear under a wisteria vine before she pulled her gaze back to the white Victorian house that had been a second home to her and her sisters since the death of their parents. Through the years it had also been a haven for her family when riding out the hurricanes that battered their shores.

She glanced at the blue sky. There was no storm today.

Instead a gentle breeze stirred the leaves on the trees in the yard and sent music from the wind chimes hanging on the back porch resonating through her weary mind. Her gaze drifted upward to the open window in the corner on the second floor. Lace curtains fluttered on the sill.

She cupped her hands around her mouth. "Hey, anybody up there?"

The curtains parted, and her twenty-two-year-old sister Betsy appeared. Her long brown hair blew around her shoulders, and the dimples in her cheeks winked with a smile before her eyebrows drew down into a scowl. She placed her hands on the windowsill and stuck her head out the opening. "It's about time you got here. Did it ever occur to you to call and let your family know you're okay? Getting shot at on the beach doesn't happen every day, and neither does finding a body."

Kate placed her hands on her hips. "I'm sorry. I've been so busy, but I figured the island hotline had broadcast all the latest news. How did you hear?"

"I stopped for coffee at the Sandwich Shop this morning, and Grady was in there."

Kate's response was cut off by a squeal accompanied by the slam of the back door. Emma, her ten-year-old sister, flew at her and grabbed her around the waist. Laughing, Kate reached down and picked up the little girl. "Oh, Emma, you're getting so heavy I can hardly lift you."

The child locked her legs around Kate, rocked back in Kate's arms and smiled. Emma's tongue peeked through the gap where a tooth had been a few days before, and Kate's heart pumped. She reached up and smoothed a strand of Emma's hair back into the ponytail that had become the hairdo of choice over the past few months.

As it did every time Kate looked into her sister's face, a lump formed in her throat. The brown eyes, so like their mother's, always sent a longing through Kate for what Emma had missed in not knowing their mother longer. But Kate had promised their mother as she was dying when Emma was only four she would take care of her sisters and her father, and that was what she'd done.

"Where have you been all day, Kate?" Without waiting for an answer, Emma tilted her head and glanced up at Betsy in the window. "Betsy has been painting all day. But guess what Treasury and I did?"

"What?"

Emma's face beamed as she wiggled out of Kate's arms. "We made my costume for the play this weekend."

"I can hardly wait to see it. I know you're going to be the prettiest girl in the play."

Emma shrugged, and her eyebrows arched. "Well, I'm only a servant girl in Blackbeard's house this year, but I'm going to have a bigger part next year."

"I'm sure you will. We've practiced your line enough to warrant a bigger speaking part next summer."

As if on cue, they leaned toward each other and spoke in unison. "More ale, sir?"

Betsy leaned farther out the window and laughed. "I've heard that so many times it's beginning to haunt me when I sleep. Emma, why don't you go see if dinner's almost ready?"

Emma glanced up at her sister and nodded. "Treasury's already told me it'll be about twenty minutes."

"Then I'll be down in a few minutes. After I eat, I have to get back to work. I'm trying to finish this last painting that I'm going to have for sale at the festival this weekend. I'll see you two in the dining room later."

Kate waved as Betsy ducked back inside. As she and Emma headed for the back door, Kate smiled down at the child. "So you've helped Treasury today? Lisa told me yesterday that she wants you to come to the station and help her with filing whenever you can."

"Oh, can I come tomorrow? I like helping at the police station." Emma's eyes blazed with excitement.

"We'll see. But I need to talk to Treasury now. Why don't you come in the house and watch TV until dinner?"

Emma pushed the back door open and scampered ahead of Kate. The smell of coffee drifted from the kitchen and reminded Kate of her interrupted lunch. She hadn't had anything since.

Treasury Wilkes turned from the sink. Her eyebrows pulled into a worried frown, and she hurried across the kitchen toward Kate. She grabbed her by the shoulders, held her at arms' length and stared into her face. "Are you all right? I was scared to death when I heard that you'd been shot at on the beach. I called the station, and Lisa told me you were okay." Her frown grew deeper. "Did you ever think about calling to let us know?"

Kate's face grew warm, and she glanced down at the floor. It was as if she was being chastised by her mother. "I'm sorry, Treasury. There was so much happening today. I'll do better in the future. I promise."

After a moment, Treasury released her. "Good. I never heard of such. People killed, police officers shot at and a bomb blowing up. What's going to happen next on our island?"

Kate shook her head. "I don't know."

"If you're through chasing criminals for the day, maybe you can do something about that cat."

Kate laughed and glanced at Emma. "He nearly scared me to death when he ran under my feet in the backyard. I think the name Rascal fits him well."

Emma's eyes grew wide. "He's my friend. I love him. He lets me count his toes. He has six."

Treasury propped her hands on her hips and arched an eyebrow. "Have you been helping that pesky prowler get in my garbage cans?"

Emma shook her head. "No. He can't get in the cans. You put those bumpy cords on them."

Kate burst out laughing and hugged Emma to her. "Not bumpy cords. They're bungee cords. Now why don't you go on and watch TV while I talk to Treasury?"

Treasury watched the child scamper away before she turned back to the oven and pulled out a pan of dinner rolls that made Kate's mouth water. Nobody on the island could cook like Treasury.

As she poured a cup of coffee, Kate regarded the frail woman who had been their mother's best friend. The years were beginning to take their toll. The responsibility of running the Island Connection Bed-and-Breakfast was becoming a burden. In addition to the busy tourist season, there were always repairs to be made on the building and hurricane season to survive. After working all her life, Treasury deserved some relief from the day-to-day worry of running her business.

With no family, the aging Treasury might soon become the responsibility of Kate and Betsy, and that was exactly how it should be. After their mother's death, Treasury was the only one Kate and Betsy could talk to about her. Their father had kept his grief to himself. Then after his death, they realized that the years had formed a lifelong commitment between all of them.

Kate dropped into a chair at the kitchen table and crossed her arms on the tabletop. "Something else happened this morning."

A small frown crinkled Treasury's forehead. "What?"

"I ran into someone on the beach." Kate leaned back in her chair and tilted her head to one side. "Someone you probably already knew was on the island. Brock Gentry. And he tells me you've invited him for dinner tonight."

Treasury picked up a towel and wiped her hands. "Yes, he's a guest here. You know I always offer my guests the option of having dinner here instead of going out. In fact I have several others that are joining us as well as Brock." Treasury leaned against the kitchen counter and directed a probing stare at Kate. "How did you feel seeing him after all these years?"

Kate shrugged. "I don't know. Confused and a little angry."

Treasury reached out and took Kate's hand in hers. "What happened between you and Brock was a long time ago. One of the hardest things to learn in a relationship is how to compromise, and neither one of you had learned that. You weren't ready for the responsibilities that come with marriage. I doubt if you would have made it."

"Do you really think so?" Kate had never thought of her heartbreak that way.

Treasury nodded. "And if you'd married him, you wouldn't have been here to take care of your family when they needed you the most. I think God knew where you needed to be at the time."

"Maybe so," Kate murmured.

Treasury placed a finger under Kate's chin and tilted her head up. "But that doesn't mean your life is over, Kate. God still has a plan for you. You just have to look for it."

Tears threatened to flood Kate's eyes, but she blinked them back. "Thanks, Treasury. I always feel better after talking to you."

Treasury put her arm around Kate's shoulders and gave her a hug. "Good. Now why don't you help me get this food on the table so we can have a nice dinner?"

Kate drained her cup of coffee and stood. "What do you need me to do?"

Fifteen minutes later Kate poured the last glass of water and stepped back to survey Treasury's specialty, a dish of baked shrimp, that bubbled in the center of the table. On the sideboard, a traditional island fig cake graced the crystal dessert plate that had belonged to Treasury's mother. Meals at the Island Connection were served family style. Treasury tried to make each guest feel as if they were more than a guest, that they were family members for a short period of time.

Kate inhaled the tempting smells of the kitchen and dining room and pressed her hand against her growling stomach. A chuckle from behind startled her, and she whirled around. Brock stood just inside the door from the hallway.

"Hungry?"

Her face warmed, and she moved to the head of the table. Bending over to straighten the napkin and silverware next to the plate, she nodded. "I missed most of my lunch."

Brock stepped into the room. "Did you find out anything about the bomb that was left?"

She opened her mouth to tell him about the conversation she'd had with the mysterious caller earlier, but she swallowed the words. For the time being, she should keep that information to herself. Her thoughts went to the teenager who'd been injured in the alley.

"The boy's parents came to the Health Center. They were very concerned about him, but they were thankful he wasn't injured worse."

Brock nodded. "He was lucky. I don't understand why anyone would leave one of those things knowing that somebody could be injured when it exploded."

"I know. It doesn't make sense to me, either."

The sound of footsteps coming down the staircase caught Kate's attention, and she glanced past Brock to the hallway. A man, who looked to be in his late thirties, stepped into the room and stopped next to Brock. He shoved his hands in the pockets of the khaki pants he wore and smiled at Kate. His eyebrows arched slightly as his gaze traveled over her uniform. He turned to Brock and grinned.

"This is your first full day on the island. Are you already in trouble with the law?"

Brock chuckled and pointed to Kate. "No, Kate and her sisters are friends of Mrs. Wilkes. They're joining us for dinner tonight." He tilted his head toward the man. "Kate, this is Dillon McAllister. He's one of Treasury's guests. And Dillon, this is Deputy Kate Michaels. She's the chief deputy on the island."

Dillon stepped toward Kate and shook her hand. "I'm pleased to meet you, Deputy Michaels. I've been on your island since day before yesterday. I can't tell you how much I'm enjoying it already."

"I'm glad you are, but please call me Kate. Are you here alone?"

He nodded. "Unfortunately, yes. My wife was supposed to come, but her mother became ill right before we left. She stayed behind to take care of her. I would have canceled the trip, but this really isn't a vacation for me. I'm here doing some research."

Kate raised her eyebrows. "Research?"

"Yes. I teach history at the University of Arkansas. I'm especially interested in the pirate activities along the eastern seaboard of the United States during the 1700s. I'm doing research about the stories of sunken ships and buried treasure in this part of the country. My department at school is allowing me some time off to gather material for the textbook that I'm writing."

Kate nodded. "Then you've come to the right place. There are all kinds of stories about the ships that lie in what's called the Graveyard of the Atlantic. Ocracoke was the headquarters for Blackbeard during that time period. He was killed in a battle just offshore, and legend has it that his treasure is buried somewhere on Ocracoke. Have you met our unofficial island historian yet?"

Dillon shook his head. "I didn't know there was one."

Kate laughed. "His name is Grady Teach. He's a descendant of Blackbeard and can tell you all kinds of stories that he says have been handed down through his family. You'll see him around the village taking tourists on walking tours to points of interests. If you want me to, I'll get in touch with him and introduce you."

"Thanks. I'd appreciate that."

"You may not be thanking me after you meet Grady. He's quite a character, and his stories can be unbelievable at times. You have to filter out the truth from the fiction. But he does have a lot of knowledge about history during that time period."

Dillon nodded. "That's what I'm looking for."

"You've also come to the island at a good time," Kate added. "This weekend we're having our annual Blackbeard Festival. There will be all kinds of activities that focus on the pirates who sailed our waters in the early 1700s. The arts and crafts community will have booths set up everywhere selling their work, and the island will be swamped with visitors from the mainland. There's a play Friday night, and my little sister Emma has a role for the first time. She can hardly wait."

Brock laughed. "She told me about it this afternoon."

Kate looked over Brock and Dillon. "You'll each have to get a costume. Everybody will be dressed as pirates."

Dillon nodded. "I bought one this afternoon. Everywhere you go in the village folks are getting ready for the festival. From the brochure I picked up in Mrs. Wilkes's entry, it looks like it's going to be a great weekend."

Before Kate could respond footsteps sounded in the hallway, and Brock glanced over his shoulder before he stepped aside for a woman dressed in tight-fitting capri pants and a low-cut silk blouse to enter the dining room. She cast a provocative smile in Brock's direction and flipped her long, blond hair back. "Well, there you are. I missed you this afternoon."

Brock's face flushed, and he cast a quick glance in Kate's direction before he answered, "I was around."

The woman arched her eyebrows and cast a glance over her shoulder at the man behind her. "Well, I spent the whole afternoon by myself. I thought I was even going to have to come to dinner alone. Sam stayed out on the water all day in that fishing boat he rented."

Kate tensed at the memory of a lone fishing skiff and a man with a pair of binoculars. She narrowed her eyes and studied the man who appeared behind his wife.

The white polo shirt he wore accented the sunburn on his face and arms. He directed an icy stare at his wife before he turned to Brock and stuck out his hand. "Women," he growled. "Tracey knows we came to Ocracoke so I could fish and she could lie on the beach. Then she complains when I spend the day doing what I want."

The woman flashed a glare at her husband, and her mouth drew into a straight line. "But we've been here three days, and so far I've only seen you at meals."

The man started to speak, but Brock cleared his throat and glanced at Kate. "Kate, I'd like you to meet Sam and Tracey Burnett. They're from Baltimore. I met them when I checked in last night." He pointed to Kate. "And this is Deputy Michaels."

Sam Burnett's face broke into a big smile, and he extended his hand. His abrupt change of demeanor reminded Kate of the car salesman on the mainland who'd tried to convince her to buy a used car that looked as if it had seen better days.

"Nice to meet you, Deputy Michaels."

Kate nodded to the two. "We're glad to have you on Ocracoke. I hope you enjoy your vacation here." A pan clattered in the kitchen, and she glanced over her shoulder. "If you'll take your seats, I'll go call my sisters to dinner and help Treasury get the rest of the food on the table."

As the group assembled around the table, Kate stepped into the hallway but turned to observe Sam and Tracey Burnett. Tracey appeared to be much younger than her husband. She sat down next to Dillon, who'd already taken a seat, and her husband took the chair beside her.

Kate's gaze raked Sam, but she could see nothing familiar about the man. That wasn't unusual, though. Whoever had been on the boat earlier had been far away, and his features had been hidden by a hooded sweatshirt. She heard nothing in his voice that reminded her of the mysterious caller at the Health Center, but that also wasn't surprising. She was sure the man had disguised his voice.

At that moment Emma bounded down the stairway with Betsy close behind. Their laughter echoed off the walls of the old house.

"I'm going to beat you to the table," Emma called out.

"Oh, no, you're not," Betsy said.

They both stopped at the foot of the steps when they spied Kate. She shook her head but couldn't suppress a grin. "Okay, you two. Try not to embarrass Treasury in front of her guests."

Emma giggled. "Okay, Kate." She glanced around at Betsy. "But I'm sitting by Brock."

Kate turned a questioning glance to Betsy as Emma ran into the dining room. "Brock said they'd met. How did that happen?"

Betsy nodded. "She talked to him for a long time this afternoon. She was playing in the backyard with Rascal when he came up. When he told her he remembered her when she was a little girl and that he knew her mother, Emma wouldn't let him out of her sight for the rest of the afternoon." Betsy reached out and grasped Kate's hand. A worried look flashed in her eyes. "Are you okay with him being here?"

Kate didn't know how to answer that. Was she okay? She didn't know yet.

She smiled and squeezed Betsy's hand. "Don't worry about me. I can take care of myself."

Betsy studied her for a moment before she cocked an eyebrow. "Can you? You carry a gun and you act tough, but underneath you're a vulnerable woman. There are some things in life that wound us so much we can't deal with them. Let me know if I can help you get through Brock's visit."

"I will." Kate glanced toward the kitchen. "Now I'd better go help Treasury with the food. You go on in the dining room."

As Kate headed to the kitchen, her cell phone rang. She pulled it from her pocket and frowned when she saw Calvin's number. She pushed the Connect button and placed the phone to her ear.

"Kate speaking."

"Hi, Kate. You'd asked me to check with Bob down at the marina about people renting boats today. When I talked with him earlier, he discovered that one of their boats was missing. I just found it tied up down by the North Ferry Terminal for Hatteras."

"Are you sure it's one of Bob's boats?"

"Yeah. All his rentals have his business name and emergency number on board. It's his, all right. I've called him to come identify it. I thought you might want to come, too."

"I'll be right there."

Kate shoved the phone back in her pocket and strode to the kitchen. Treasury picked up a tray of dinner rolls as Kate walked in. Her eyes widened. "What's the matter?"

"Something's come up. I have to go. I'll eat when I get back."

Treasury nodded. "Okay. I know better than to argue with you when duty calls. I'll keep your dinner warm."

Kate leaned over and kissed Treasury on the cheek. "What would I do without you? I'll be back later."

"Where are you going?" Brock's voice from the doorway startled Kate, and she turned toward him.

"Calvin called. I have to go."

He stepped closer. "Does this have anything to do with that bottle bomb earlier today?"

She shrugged. "Maybe. I'm not sure."

"Where are you going?"

"I have to meet Calvin out at the North Ferry Terminal."

Brock frowned. "That's fourteen miles from here. What's out there?"

Kate shook her head. "I really can't talk to you about this. It's—"

"Police business," Brock finished for her. "I know, but I'm a policeman, Kate. And you can tell me what you know. I only want to help."

Kate hesitated for a moment. She'd never had a day before as busy as this one had been, and she knew Calvin and Doug were just as tired as she was. Maybe she did need someone to bounce theories off—and who better to do that with than a man who dealt with police investigations every day?

She took a deep breath. "All right. You can go with me. On the way I'll fill you in on the man aboard the fishing skiff at the beach this morning." She hurried to the dining-room door. "Treasury, would you keep Brock's supper warm, too? He's going with me."

Tracey Burnett had just taken a drink of water, and she set her glass back down and directed a disappointed glance at Brock before she smiled and turned her attention to Dillon

McAllister sitting next to her. Betsy frowned at Kate and shook her head.

Kate didn't have time to deal with her sister's concern right now. Calvin and Doug both looked to her for guidance on a day-to-day basis. Although she loved her job, sometimes it became a rather lonely position. The sheriff was too far away to give her much help. It would be good to have someone she could talk to on a professional basis.

The fact that it was Brock wasn't going to bother her. She could accept his help and not let it dredge up memories from the past. Right now all she wanted was to find Jake's killer and identify the shooter on the beach. She only hoped that would also lead her to the bottle bomber and the man who promised that he'd be seeing her.

If not, she might need more help than even Brock Gentry could offer.

FIVE

As the squad car rolled along the two-lane road toward the North Ferry Terminal, Brock listened to Kate relate the experience she'd had at the crime scene on the beach earlier in the day. When she'd finished, he bit down on his lip and thought about what she'd said.

He swiveled in his seat to face her. "Do you think the man in the boat might have had something to do with the murder on the beach?"

"I don't think so. He sounded like he didn't know who I was talking about when I asked him if he killed Jake."

Brock thought he must have misunderstood her. He leaned closer. "You lost me with that last statement. You asked him if he killed Jake? When?"

"Oh, I haven't told you that part. The man who claimed to have left the bomb called the Health Center while I was there checking on the injured boy."

Brock's concerns grew with each word as Kate related her conversation with the man on the phone. "He may not be connected to Jake's murder, but this guy sounds like he has something else planned. I never would have thought police work on this quiet island would be so involved. Is it always like this?"

Kate laughed. "No, thank goodness. We've never had a day like this."

The North Terminal came into view. Cars lined the boarding lane waiting for the next ferry that would take them to the neighboring island of Hatteras. Brock scanned the back area of the terminal for a police car. "Do you see your officer anywhere?"

Kate pointed to a car sitting at the back of the parking lot and drove toward it. "There he is." She pulled to a stop beside Calvin's squad car and groaned. "Oh, no. I'd forgotten Mike Thornton is working at the marina this summer."

"Is that bad?" Brock asked.

"Only if his father shows up. Ean Thornton thinks his son does no wrong. I've had plenty of experience dealing with that."

"Spoiled kid, huh?"

Kate nodded. "When Mike was about three years old, he was playing near where his father was cleaning some fish he'd caught that day. When Ean turned his back, Mike picked up a boning knife and fell with it in his hand. It sliced his cheek open from near his earlobe toward his nose. Ean's always felt guilty for leaving the knife where Mike could get it. I don't think he's ever corrected Mike for anything he's done since then."

Taking a deep breath, she climbed from the car and Brock followed, his gaze taking in the scene before him. Three men in shorts and white T-shirts stood near Calvin. Their sun visors sported the monogrammed logo of Bob's Marine Rentals. Brock assumed that the older of the three was Bob. The other two looked like college students.

A young man with a bored expression on his face leaned against the fender of Calvin's squad car with his arms crossed. His lip curled into a half smile as they approached, and the faint scar on his cheek wrinkled. He touched two fingers to the bill of his sun visor in a casual salute. "Evening, Deputy Michaels."

"Hello, Mike. Good to see you."

The boy chuckled and directed a smirk in their direction. "Yeah, I'll bet."

Another young man, his hands in the pockets of his cutoff jeans, stood to the side and rocked back and forth from one foot to the other. Freckles dotted the gangly boy's face, and his curly red hair stuck out underneath his sun visor.

Brock smiled at him, but the boy didn't seem to notice. His attention appeared to be riveted on the man in deep conversation with Calvin. "Now, Bob," Brock heard Calvin say, "you need to calm down. You've got your boat back."

"Do you have any idea how much a rig like that costs?" He accented his words by pointing toward a fishing boat that sat tied to a small dock behind the terminal. They turned as Kate stopped beside them. Brock eased up behind her.

"I imagine quite a bit, but…" Calvin halted in midsentence and stared past Kate at Brock. A surprised look flashed across his face. "Mr. Gentry, you seem to be showing up at all our crime scenes lately."

Brock shook his head. "A policeman can't stand to be out of the loop when there's trouble around, but I just rode along with Kate tonight."

Kate didn't elaborate on Brock's presence. Instead she directed her attention back to Calvin. "How did you find the boat?"

Calvin inclined his head toward the ferry station. "One of the workers spotted it out here and called the station."

"Did anybody over there see the person who left it?"

"No. I questioned all of them before you got here. They said they were so busy all day they didn't see anything."

Kate pursed her lips and stared at the road back to Ocracoke Village and then toward the inlet to Hatteras. "The thief could have gotten on the ferry as a passenger or hitch-hiked back to the village. Either way it'll be surprising if we find him." After a moment she turned back to the man who'd been talking with Calvin. "Hi, Bob. I'm glad your missing boat turned up. When did you first realize it was gone?"

Bob glanced over at the two young men who hadn't moved. He jabbed a finger in the redheaded boy's direction. "Hey, Kyle, come over here and tell Kate what happened this morning." The boy glanced at Mike, who hadn't moved, and trudged over to stand by Bob. "This is Kyle Johnson, Russell Johnson's grandson. He's visiting the island this summer, and his grandfather asked me to give him a job. He was at the marina this morning."

"What happened, Kyle?" Kate asked.

Kyle stared down at the ground, but he darted a glance to Mike before he spoke. "Mike and I were supposed to open up this morning. When I got there, Mike called on my cell phone and said he was running a little late and would be there as soon as he could."

"Were you there by yourself?"

"Yes, and before I knew it I had people waiting everywhere, and all of them wanting to leave right away. I saw this guy standing over to the side like he was waiting for a boat. But by the time I'd taken care of everybody, he was gone. I figured he gave up and left. But I guess he must have gotten the keys off the Peg-Board when I wasn't looking. There were so many people getting in boats, I didn't notice him leave."

"This man you saw waiting, can you tell me what he looked like?"

Kyle's Adam's apple bobbed, and sympathy for the boy's situation filled Brock. The kid looked scared to death. Kyle took a deep breath. "He had his back turned. All I saw was the hooded sweatshirt he was wearing."

Kate's eyes widened. "So you never saw his face. Can

you give me an idea about his size? Was he short, tall, thin, heavy?"

"He was an average-size person." The boy's face crumpled, and he turned toward Bob. "I'm sorry that I messed up, Bob, and I promise I'll be more careful in the future if you'll give me another chance. I really need this summer job." Brock thought Kyle would burst into tears any second.

Bob's gruff manner melted, and he took a deep breath. "It's okay, Kyle. We've got the boat back." He turned to glare at Mike. "No thanks to Mike. If he'd been at work on time, we wouldn't have had this problem."

Kate glanced over her shoulder at Mike. "How about joining us, Mike? I'd like to ask you a few questions."

The boy sighed, pushed away from leaning on the car, and swaggered toward them. "I called my dad to come out here," he mumbled.

Brock tensed for Kate's response, but if she heard, she gave no indication. She glanced at Bob. "We're glad your boat is recovered." She turned to Mike. "Can you add anything that might help us find out who took the boat?"

Mike shrugged. "How should I know? I wasn't even there."

Bob's face turned red, and he gritted his teeth. "You should have been. I ought to fire you."

Anger flashed across Mike's face, and he clenched his fists. He took a step toward Bob but stopped as a car skidded to a stop in the parking lot. A man jumped from inside and strode across the parking lot. His hair was a shade lighter than the red that colored his cheeks, and his muscular body reminded Brock of a bulldozer plowing ahead determined to mow down everything in its path. He doubled his fist and shook it in Kate's direction as he approached.

"Okay, Kate, what are you accusing my son of this time?"

Kate waited until the man reached her before she spoke. "Hello, Ean. I wondered if you'd show up. Nobody's accusing

Mike of anything. We're trying to get some information about a boat that was taken from the marina this morning."

Ean shook his finger at Bob. "I don't know why you don't lose one every day. I've told you that you're no kind of a businessman. You should give up and go to the mainland and get a job."

Bob took a step toward Ean, but Calvin put a restraining hand on his arm. Bob relaxed and took a deep breath. "Look, Ean, I gave your son a job for the summer as a favor to you, but it's not working out. I spend half my time covering up his mistakes. This time he came to work late and left us short-handed."

Ean's face grew redder. "He wasn't feeling well this morning. He needed some extra rest."

Kate held up her hand. "We don't have time for you two to argue." She glanced at Mike. "Why don't you go on home with your dad? I'll call you if I need anything else."

Ean glared at her. "You call *me* if you need to talk to my son, Kate. You got that straight?"

Ean clamped his hand down on Mike's shoulder and turned him toward the car. They strode across the parking lot without a backward glance.

Kate waited until they'd left before she turned to Bob. "Ean will be okay after he's cooled off."

Bob nodded. "I know. We've been friends since we started school. He goes kind of wild when he thinks someone is accusing his son of something. I'll talk to him tomorrow."

"And what about Mike?"

Bob watched Ean's car roar from the parking lot before he spoke. "Oh, I'll keep him on for the rest of the summer. I thought a few months of hard work might help keep him out of trouble, but I don't know if it will or not." He glanced at Kate. "You've had your own run-ins with him. Ean still blames you for Mike losing his driver's license."

Kate sighed. "I know. But Mike's to blame for getting those DUIs."

"Tell that to Ean."

"I've tried." She glanced toward the boat. "I'm going to leave Calvin here to see if he can lift any fingerprints off the boat. As soon as he's finished, you can take it back to the marina."

"Okay."

Kyle had remained quiet during the confrontation with Mike and his father. Now he stepped next to Bob and took a deep breath. "What about me? Are you going to fire me?"

"No, but in the future call me if Mike doesn't show up, and I'll come right down. Mornings this time of year are too busy for one person to handle." He pointed toward his car in the parking lot. "You can drive my car back to the village and leave it at the marina. I'll bring the boat."

"Okay. I'll see you in the morning."

As Kyle pulled from the lot, Kate walked over to where Brock waited. "I'll help Calvin search the boat, then I'll be ready to go back," she said.

"Take your time. I'll wait on the dock for you. I don't want to get in your way."

He followed her to the shore and onto the dock that reached out into the water. He leaned against one of the pilings and watched as she stepped onboard the boat. A breeze blew in from the ocean, and he breathed in the salt air. The memory returned of Kate's mother telling him how special her island was. At the time he couldn't wait to get away. Now he'd come back, and what he'd found disturbed him.

He'd worked enough cases to know that you never discounted any threat. From what Kate had told him about the call she'd taken at the Health Center, somebody sounded determined to cause problems. The fact that he'd ended the conversation with a promise to see Kate again concerned Brock most of all.

He had asked her earlier if she had any enemies on the island, and she'd said no. Now he wasn't so sure. Ean Thornton seemed to harbor anger against Kate for what he thought was an ongoing persecution of his son. Could Ean be the one wanting to harm Kate?

If someone was targeting her, he intended to help find out who it was. He would do everything in his power to see that she wasn't hurt. After all, he owed her that much. And he owed it to her mother to see that her daughter remained safe.

Kate stepped aboard the boat and looked around. Nothing appeared out of place. She'd seen tourists bring their rentals back to Bob's place, and usually there was trash left over from a day at sea. Not on this boat. Not even a candy wrapper lay on the floor. Whoever had taken it had either cleaned up well after himself or he wasn't in the boat for a very long period of time.

The skiff she'd seen this morning had been too far away to make a positive identification, but she was sure this was the same one. The shape and the size appeared identical to what she'd observed through the lens of her binoculars.

"What do you make of this?" Bob's voice caught her attention.

She took a step toward him. "What is it?"

Calvin gave a soft whistle. "You might want to take a look at this, Kate."

The two men stood side by side looking down at the ship's steering console. They parted to make room for her. Her mouth opened in surprise as she spied an envelope with her name on it taped to the wheel.

Kate leaned closer and studied the block letter writing.

It looked as if it could have been written by any third-grade child. She glanced up at Calvin. "Hand me a pair of gloves out of the equipment bag."

He opened the bag and held out the box that contained latex gloves. Kate pulled them on and lifted the envelope. The flap of the envelope was stuffed inside, and she carefully pulled it out. She then extracted the single sheet of paper from inside and dropped the envelope in the plastic bag Calvin held.

Bob and Calvin leaned forward as she unfolded the sheet of paper. She gasped when she read the short message written, then held it out for Calvin to get a better view.

Calvin's face blanched. "Oh, my."

"What is it? What have you found?"

Kate looked around at Brock, who had climbed onboard. "I thought you were going to wait on the dock," she said.

He shook his head. "Sorry. I couldn't stay back. What did you find?"

She held up the note. "My mysterious caller has now left me a message."

Brock squinted at the letter in her hand. "What does it say?"

Kate took a deep breath and dropped her gaze to the note. "It says—*Dear Kate, do you know the 'Somebody Done Somebody Wrong' song? If you don't, you will soon.*"

The muscle in Brock's jaw twitched, and he shook his head. "I don't like this, Kate. First this guy uses a song title to let you know he's going to be seeing you, then he sends a message that sounds like he has a grudge against you. Can you think of anybody that might want to harm you?"

She thought for a moment. "No. If I have any enemies on Ocracoke, I don't know about it." She glanced at Calvin. "Can you think of anybody that might want to target me?"

"Of course not. Everybody loves you, Kate. I've never heard one person say a bad thing about you."

Brock directed a piercing stare at her. "Think of people you've arrested in the past. Maybe someone who went to prison. Is there any one of them who might secretly be waiting to get even?"

She shook her head. "The only one I've arrested that spent any time in jail is Jake. But he's dead."

"Then maybe it's one of his friends. It could even be the guy on the phone."

Kate thought about that. "But he acted like he didn't know Jake."

"He could have been trying to throw you off his trail. It seems likely that they're the same person. You've had a murder and an exploding bomb today. What are the odds of having two serious crimes committed by different people in a day's time on Ocracoke?"

Calvin spoke up. "Not very big." He turned to Kate. "I think Brock may be right, Kate."

She sighed and dropped the note in the bag with the envelope. "I think so, too. But there's nothing we can do about it now. Let's finish up here. It looks like the thief cleaned up after himself well. If he wiped everything down, we probably won't find a fingerprint anywhere. Even if we did, it could be from anybody who's rented the boat before. Right now what we could use is a good lead."

Calvin glanced at Kate. "Why don't you and Brock go on? I'll finish up here and get back on duty. I'll let you know if anything comes up tonight."

"Are you sure you're going to be all right? You were on duty last night, and you came in this morning."

Calvin waved his hand in dismissal. "I slept a few hours on the cot in the back room at the station this afternoon. So I'll be all right."

"You call if you need me," Kate said.

"I will. Go on now." Calvin turned and picked up the evidence bag.

Kate stepped onto the dock, and Brock followed. As she walked back to the squad car, she watched the vehicles boarding the ferry to Hatteras. Carloads of tourists arrived and left the island each day. When you added all the visitors to the year-round residents, there were thousands of people driving and walking around Ocracoke on any given day in the summer. Now one of them held a grudge against her.

She had no idea who it might be, but she knew she had to find him before Treasury and her sisters found out about the threats. They would insist she leave the island and turn the investigation over to Sheriff Baxter. She couldn't do that.

She glanced at Brock walking beside her. She'd been upset when she saw him on the beach. Now, as much as she hated to admit it, she was glad he was here. For the first time in years she didn't feel alone. She needed a good investigator, and Brock was that, all right. She just had to make sure she didn't let her feelings go any further.

SIX

An hour later Brock and Kate sat on the wraparound back porch of the bed-and-breakfast at one of the white wicker tables where Treasury's guests ate breakfast. Their empty plates sat on the table, and the small hurricane lamp in the center of the table cast a yellow glow in the dark night.

Brock tilted his head and listened. "It's so peaceful here. It's really different from Nashville."

Kate took a sip of coffee from the cup she held, settled back in her chair and glanced at Brock. He'd been quiet since they left the ferry terminal. She crossed her legs and gazed into the darkness. "It makes today almost seem like a dream."

He glanced at her. "How long has it been since you've had as many incidents as you had today?"

"I can't remember a day like this. When the tourists are here, we usually have some drunks, and we've had some drug problems, but nothing like today."

He put his hands behind his head, stretched his legs out in front of him and scooted down into the chair. He closed his eyes for a moment. "In my job, it's worse than this for me every day."

"I can imagine. It stands to reason that a city would have more crime. But that's what you wanted."

He sighed. "Yeah, I did, and I got what I wanted."

They sat in silence for a moment before Kate spoke again. "Did you get enough to eat?"

He chuckled and reached down to pat his stomach. "I don't know if it's the sea air or if I haven't had any good home cooking in a while, but that baked shrimp was delicious. Do you and your sisters eat here often?"

"Every chance we get. My job keeps me busy, and Betsy's paintings of Ocracoke wildlife and landscapes are in high demand by tourists now. She's also getting ready for a showing in an art gallery in Raleigh. So that leaves little time for cooking, and Treasury enjoys having us here. She takes care of Emma, and Emma follows her everywhere. I think Emma may turn out to be the best cook in the family."

Brock pushed up to a sitting position in his chair before he swiveled and stared at her. "You've built a good life here with your sisters, Kate. I'm happy for you."

Her skin warmed at the piercing stare he directed at her. She picked up her cup and took another drink. "Thank you, Brock. And I'm happy you've reconnected with your father."

"So am I. When I was growing up, I couldn't understand why my father left us. My mother wouldn't talk to me about him, and I thought it was my fault he'd gone away. Then during my teenage years, I told myself I hated him, but it wasn't true. No matter how hard I tried to deny it, I knew I still loved him and wanted to know him."

"I heard you say you hated him many times, but I wondered if you really did."

Brock nodded. "I realized the truth when I walked into that hospital room and saw him near death. I wanted him to live more than I've ever wanted anything. He opened his eyes, and the first thing he did was ask for my forgiveness. He said he left because he was an alcoholic and thought my mother and I would be better off without him. Five years ago, he ended up in a homeless shelter, and they helped him overcome his alcoholism."

"Why didn't he contact you then?"

"I asked him that, and he said he thought I probably didn't want to see him. It was the director of the shelter who called me about the accident. He thought I should know, and I'm thankful for that."

"Does your mother know what has happened?"

"Yes. I love my mother, but she's remarried and lives in New Jersey. I don't see her very often. Now that my father's back in my life, I'm beginning to see how important family can be. I'm sorry I didn't understand that six years ago."

Kate's heart thudded, and she took a deep breath. "It *is* important. Betsy, Emma and I are fortunate to have each other, but there's something missing."

He turned a questioning gaze toward her. "What?"

She took another sip of coffee before she answered. "Right before my father died, he told us something that we'd never known. He said that when he was a young man, he left Ocracoke to work on the mainland. He met a woman, married her and had a son."

"You have a brother?"

"Yes. My father's first wife died soon after their son was born, and her sister offered to help him care for the baby. When the baby was nearly a year old, Dad decided to come back to Ocracoke. His sister-in-law became upset that he was going to take his son away from her. One day when he was at work, she took the boy, whose name was Scott, and disappeared. The police looked everywhere for her, but it was no use. It was like she had disappeared into thin air."

Brock's eyes were wide. "Wow. That must have been tough."

"It was. After several months, my father moved back here. He'd dated my mother before he moved away, and they renewed their relationship and married. But he never gave up trying to find Scott. That was his greatest disappointment—that he was dying without knowing what happened to his son."

"So do you and your sisters still want to find him?"

"Yes. We've searched on the internet for the past three years, but we haven't been able to find anything. But then, we're not sure where to search. We don't know if his name is still Scott Michaels or if his aunt changed it. He probably has no idea we even exist. But we feel that there's a piece of our family missing, and we won't be satisfied until we find him."

Brock leaned forward and crossed his arms on top of the wicker table. "Then why not hire a private investigator?"

Kate laughed. "Because they cost a lot of money, and we don't have any. Besides we don't have anything that might help. His aunt even took his birth certificate."

Brock thought for a moment. "I have a friend in Nashville who is a private investigator. He's a master at finding missing relatives. He owes me a favor. Would you like for me to ask him to see what he could find out?"

Kate reached across the table and covered his hand with hers. "Oh, Brock, would you? This means so much to me, and we'd be grateful for anything he could do."

He looked down at her hand on his, then placed his other one on top of hers. "I'll call him tomorrow. I'll do anything I can to help you find your brother, Kate."

Kate stiffened at the tone of his voice. How many times in the past had they sat with his hands wrapped around hers when they talked of their future? A sinking feeling started in the pit of her stomach and rose to her throat.

What was she doing? Yesterday she only had bitter memories of Brock Gentry. Tonight she sat on Treasury's back porch holding hands with him. She couldn't be drawn in by him again. He would only hurt her like he had before.

Kate jerked her hand loose and pushed to her feet. She stumbled backward, knocking her chair to the floor. "I told you that I would help you with your problems while you were on the island, but that doesn't mean we can ever go back to where we were. I appreciate your help today, and I will be forever grateful if your friend can find my brother. But that's as far as it will ever go with us. Do you understand?"

He rose and faced her. "I'm sorry, Kate. The good meal and the moonlight is probably to blame for my momentary lapse in judgment. I respect how you feel, and it won't happen again."

She took a deep breath. "Good. Now I need to get home. Betsy and Emma left while we were at the ferry, and I need to check on them. Maybe I'll see you tomorrow."

She turned toward the porch steps, but he stepped around her and blocked her way. "Is it all right if I come by your office and bring Dillon? He seems eager to meet your island historian."

She hesitated before she answered. "Come about ten. I'll have Grady there."

"See you then."

Kate turned and hurried down the back steps to her squad car parked in the driveway. When she climbed inside, she cranked the engine and looked back at Brock. He still stood where she left him.

She put the car in gear and headed for home. As she drove through the village, she watched the tourists who still walked along the streets or rode bicycles. She pulled to a stop at a crosswalk and waited for a group of college-age kids to walk in front of her car. They were laughing, and it reminded her of another lifetime when she and Brock were that young.

Kate glanced down at her hand on the steering wheel. It

burned as if Brock's touch had seared her skin. She raised her arm and flexed her fingers. For a moment tonight she had almost forgotten. Almost, but not quite.

Brock Gentry was a part of her past, and she would never let her guard down again with him. She had loved him once, and it had left deep scars on her heart that were just now beginning to fade. She couldn't take a chance on reopening them.

Kate glanced at the clock on the squad car's dash the next morning as she pulled to a stop at the ramp leading to the spot on the beach where Jake's body had been discovered. Nine o'clock. She had time to check out the beach before she met Brock and Dillon. She climbed out and walked toward the National Park Service truck that sat beside the road. Clay Phillips, the park ranger in charge of the island lighthouse, stood next to it.

"Morning, Clay. How are you?"

A hammer dangled from his hand. He raised it and pointed toward the large sign sticking in the ground at the entrance to the beach.

WARNING—RIP CURRENTS
SWIM AT OWN RISK

"I'm good. Had to put out the signs."

Kate glanced toward the large waves crashing on the seashore. Their high-energy surge provided the perfect circumstances to spawn the deadly currents that claimed too many lives on the Outer Banks. "Surf's really up."

Clay pointed down the beach. "Yeah, and would you just look at that?"

Chairs, some covered by large umbrellas, dotted the beach where groups had claimed their territory for the day. Several children played in the surf, and a group of teenagers batted a volleyball back and forth over a net.

Kate inclined her head in the direction of the sun worshippers. "Do they know about the currents?"

Clay's mouth thinned into a straight line. "I told each group, but it didn't do any good." He shook his head in disgust. "I'll never understand why people ignore our warnings."

Kate nodded and turned her attention to the ocean and the huge waves that crashed then rippled over the sand. One after another they washed across the area where Jake's body had been found. She pointed to the spot. "That's where we found Jake's body yesterday."

Clay opened the toolbox in the back of his truck and tossed the hammer inside. "I know all about it."

Kate chuckled. "You've heard, huh?"

Clay's tanned face broke into a big grin. "Yeah. I stopped at the Sandwich Shop yesterday to get my morning coffee. Grady was having a great time holding court while he gave all the details of his morning adventure." He placed his hands on his hips and leaned against the tailgate of his truck. "Are you looking for evidence?"

Kate shrugged. "No. Just wanted to revisit the scene of the crime, I guess. Were you on the beach any yesterday?"

"No. I was on duty at the lighthouse all day."

Kate smiled at the thought of the island lighthouse, which dated to the early 1800s. The lighthouse, the oldest one in North Carolina, was the most beloved structure on the island and still functioned as a navigational tool for ships. "I imagine you're staying busy with tours for visitors now."

He stared at her, and a warning triggered in Kate's mind. He shook his head. "I'm never too busy for you, Kate. I keep hoping that one of these days you're going to break down and go out with me."

She tried to meet his gaze, but she couldn't. She turned and stared down the beach. "Maybe. But I have a murder case to solve right now."

Clay straightened and shoved his hands in his pockets. "Yeah, you've always got some excuse. Well, I'm not going to detain you any longer. If you change your mind, you know where to find me."

"Bye, Clay."

She turned and hurried down to the beach where a group of teenage girls lay sprawled on beach towels soaking up the sun. "Hey, girls," she said, "we've got riptides today. I'd stay out of the water if I were you."

They raised their heads and stared at her through sunglass-covered eyes before they nodded and lay back down. Kate walked a little farther down the beach but glanced over her shoulder toward the road. She could still see Clay's truck parked in front of her squad car. What was taking him so long to leave? Had she made him angry?

Ever since he'd come to the island six months ago, he'd tried to get her to go out with him. At first he'd been very insistent, but he hadn't seemed as interested lately. She'd hoped he'd found someone else to focus on. Maybe she'd been wrong.

As she watched, the truck roared to life and pulled away from the beach ridge. She watched the truck disappear and she turned back to look at the ocean. The water looked rough this morning. There were no fishing boats in sight. At least she wasn't being observed like yesterday.

After stopping to talk to each group on the beach and warn them of the dangers, she headed back to her car. She stopped at the top of the beach ramp several minutes later and gazed over the sandy expanse once more before she walked past the dunes. It was hard to believe that just yesterday a man had been murdered in the tranquil setting.

Giving the beach area one last glance, she trudged toward her car. Perspiration dotted her brow from the hot sun overhead. It was getting late, and she'd told Brock she'd meet him and Dillon at the station at ten o'clock.

Kate opened the door of the squad car and was about to climb in when she saw something. She closed her eyes for a moment and reopened them to make sure she wasn't imagining the envelope taped to the steering wheel of her squad car. Her name in large block letters stood out on its surface like a blinking neon sign.

She reached for the envelope but drew back. Don't touch it without gloves on, she thought. A box of latex gloves sat in her trunk, and within minutes she had pulled on a pair. Carefully extracting the note from the steering wheel, she pulled the flap from inside the envelope and removed a single sheet of paper. Her heart pumped, and her eyes grew wide at the words printed on the paper.

Kate, I got this close to you, and I can do it again. Enjoy Every Breath You Take. It may be your last.

She jerked the gun from the holster on her belt and whirled to scan the surrounding area. No one on the beach appeared to be watching her, and there was no one else visible up or down the road. Her hand trembled, and she struggled to keep a grip on the gun.

She bit down on her lip and forced herself to think rationally. If he'd intended to harm her, he would already have made his move. Since he hadn't shown himself, he probably only wanted to frighten her. Was he watching and laughing at how scared she looked? If he was, she wouldn't give him the satisfaction of knowing how terrified she really was.

Kate shoved her gun back in her holster and stuck the note in her pants pocket. Then with an indifference she didn't feel, she reached in her shirt pocket, pulled out her sunglasses and slipped them on. She straightened to her full height and peered around again. Her heart pounded with fear that any minute, a bullet might cut through her, but she didn't flinch.

With one last look over her shoulder, she climbed in the squad car and cranked the engine. Her fingers tightened on the steering wheel as she slowly pulled onto the road that led into the village. She held her breath waiting for the crack of a rifle.

When she reached the edge of the town, she exhaled, pulled to the side of the road and wiped the perspiration from her forehead. Then she leaned her head on the steering wheel and offered a prayer of thanks to God for His protection.

SEVEN

Brock stepped into the police station and walked to the desk where the young woman he'd met yesterday sat. Lisa was what Kate had called her. She looked up from her computer and smiled. Her blue eyes sparkled, and her blond ponytail swayed back and forth as she nodded in his direction. "Hi, Mr. Gentry. Kate told me you were coming in this morning. She's gone out to the beach, but she'll be back in a few minutes. You can sit in here with me, or you can wait in her office."

He walked over and stopped beside her desk. "I'm expecting someone else to meet us here, so I'll wait out here with you." He inclined his head toward the two-way radio on her desk. "Any emergencies this morning?"

She smiled and shook her head. "Not like yesterday."

His gaze took in the dispatch equipment on her desk. "Let's hope not. Do you get many emergency calls?"

"We have some, but not as many as you might think with the numbers of tourists that are here. Most of the residents on the island know our phone number and call us if they have a problem. Grady did that yesterday when he found Jake's body, but tourists always call 911. Our 911 terminal is on the mainland at Swan Quarter. Any call to 911 from Ocracoke goes directly there, and they relay the emergency to us."

"Well, maybe it'll stay as quiet all day as it is now." Brock shoved his hands in his pockets and looked around for a chair. "I'll sit over here out of your way until Kate gets here."

He'd hardly gotten seated before the door opened, and Kate hurried in. She glanced at him and stopped beside Lisa's desk. He had dreaded seeing her today after their parting last night. She still appeared upset.

She spoke to Lisa for a moment, then turned to him. "Brock, can I see you a moment in my office?"

He took a deep breath and pushed to his feet. "Sure." His feet felt like they were weighted with lead as he followed her. His pulse raced, and he steeled himself for what he knew was about to happen. She was about to tell him she couldn't do what he'd asked.

She led the way into her office and moved aside for him to enter. When he'd stepped inside, she closed the door behind her and motioned to a chair. "Have a seat."

Brock took a step toward her. Red lines streaked the whites of her eyes, and even her tan couldn't hide the paleness of her face. If her pallor was caused by concern over his presence on the island, he would leave. She had enough to worry about without adding an old boyfriend to her plate.

He opened his mouth to tell her he was going to leave, but she spoke first. "Something happened this morning."

Her chin trembled, and he realized that whatever was wrong had nothing to do with his being on Ocracoke. "What?"

As he listened to her relate her trip out to the beach and finding the note in her car, fear boiled up in his throat. He struggled to keep her from seeing how concerned he was. "Did you see anybody around your car?"

"Only Clay. His truck was parked in front of my car. I thought it took him a long time to leave, but I assumed he was taking care of something in his truck."

"Yeah," Brock grunted. "Something like taping an envelope to your steering wheel. Tell me what you know about this park ranger."

Kate shrugged. "Not very much. He was transferred to the island about six months ago from the Smoky Mountain National Park. He grew up in northern Virginia. His parents and sisters still live there. He was married briefly and has a son five years old who lives with his ex-wife near Washington. He doesn't get to see him very often."

A twinge of jealousy coursed through Brock. "It sounds like you know more than a little about him. Are you dating him?"

Kate's eyes grew wide. "Dating him?"

"Yes. Are you in a relationship with him?"

Her mouth dropped open, and her eyes narrowed. She tossed the bag containing the note on her desk. "No, I'm not in a relationship with him, even though he's tried his best to change my mind. But I don't have time for that."

Brock struggled to keep the relief that Kate wasn't involved with someone else from showing on his face. "So he could be upset with you because you've rejected him."

Surprise flashed on her face. "Do you think it's possible he's the one who left the note?"

"He could be. You said yesterday that you couldn't think of anybody who might be an enemy. A rejected suitor might decide to try some payback. So might a father who blames you for causing his son legal problems."

"Do you think the man who left the notes could either be Clay or Ean?"

"I don't know. I'm just saying maybe you need to look closer at the people around you."

Kate sank down into the chair behind her desk, picked up the plastic bag and studied it a moment before she looked at him.

Her eyes held a stricken look. "This is a death threat, Brock. I can't believe either Clay or Ean would want to kill me."

He wanted to put his arms around her and assure her that she was right, but he had no idea if she was or not. "Don't worry, Kate. We're going to find this guy. I'll help you any way I can."

Her lips trembled. "Thank you. I'm trying to keep a professional attitude about this, but it's different when it seems like someone is carrying out a vendetta on you and you have no idea who it could be."

Brock smiled. "You're a police officer, Kate, but it's also okay to be human. If you weren't concerned, I'd worry about you. It's that fear that's going to help us find this guy."

Kate inhaled and pushed to her feet. She picked up a manila folder that lay on her desk and held it out to him. "I brought this from home for you."

"What is it?"

"It's all the information I have on my brother—his name, date of birth, his mother's and our father's names, hospital where he was born, his aunt's name and where our father worked and lived. It doesn't seem like much to go on, but it's all I have."

He opened the folder and rifled through the loose-leaf papers inside. "This looks good. I'll fax all this to my friend and then put it in the mail. You'd be surprised how many people he's found with a lot less to go on."

Her gaze softened. "I appreciate your help on this, Brock. It means a lot to our family."

A knock on the door interrupted his response. Lisa's voice called out from the other side. "Kate, Grady and Dillon McAllister are here."

Brock turned, opened the door and waited for Kate to exit before he followed her into the outer office. Grady, in cutoff jeans and a straw hat, stood next to Dillon. He laughed and poked a finger in Dillon's chest.

"Yes, sir, you done come to the right place if you want to know about Blackbeard. I know all about my ancestor."

Kate stopped beside Dillon and laughed. "I see you've already met Grady."

"Yep. And I'll take good care of him, Kate." Grady's wide grin revealed a missing tooth.

Kate cocked an eyebrow at Grady and wiggled a finger at him. "Remember, Grady, he wants factual information. None of your made-up stories about Blackbeard. Okay? We don't want the students who use Dillon's textbook to get the wrong information."

Grady's chest swelled, and his mouth puckered into a grimace. "I never tell anything but the gospel truth. This morning we're going out in the salt marsh to look for Blackbeard's money tree."

"Money tree?" Dillon glanced from Kate to Grady.

Grady rocked back on his heels and stuck his hands in his pockets. "Well, you see, young feller, before Blackbeard died, he buried his treasure somewhere on this island, and he promised that he would protect it. People have been tryin' to find it for years."

"You don't say." Dillon tried to suppress a grin as he glanced at Kate.

Grady's eyes sparkled as they did each time he began to spin a tale about his famous ancestor. He inched closer to Dillon. "There's them of us who believe old Blackbeard's ghost is still a-walkin' around this island just waitin' to take revenge on anybody tryin' to steal his treasure."

"Grady." Kate arched an eyebrow. "I said stick to the truth."

Dillon threw back his head and laughed. "I can see I'm in for a treat. Let's get going. I can hardly wait."

With his arm draped around Dillon's shoulders, Grady flashed a grin at Kate as they left the office. When they'd gone, Kate turned back to Lisa and started to say something but stopped. A frown covered Lisa's face. Kate stepped closer to her desk. "What's the matter, Lisa?"

She bit down on her lip and shook her head. "Maybe it's nothing, but I'm worried about Doug. He signed in for his shift nearly four hours ago and went out on patrol about thirty minutes later. I haven't heard from him since."

"Have you tried to call him?"

"I have, but he's not answering his cell phone."

"Is that unusual?" Brock asked.

Kate nodded. "Very much so. Doug always stays in touch. See if you can get him again."

Lisa picked up her cell phone, but before she could dial, the emergency radio crackled. "Nine-one-one emergency. Deputies and EMS needed on Pirate Creek Road past Swanson's Camp Ground. Officer down."

Lisa's eye widened as she reached for the mic and punched a button. "Ten-four. Officer on the way."

"Doug!" Kate almost screamed the name before she bolted and ran for the door, with Brock right behind.

He barely had time to jump into the squad car before Kate pulled away from the curb with the siren wailing. Brock glanced at her as she sped through the village and onto the road that led to the remote campground. An anguished expression covered her face.

She looked over at him. "He's just a boy, Brock. He hasn't learned how to be careful yet."

Brock wanted to reach over and touch her arm, but he didn't dare. "It's going to be all right, Kate."

She stared straight ahead. He could only see her profile, but from her stony expression he knew she was preparing herself for tragic news. "No, it's not. I have a horrible feeling that something bad has happened to Doug."

Kate sped through the village streets and swerved onto the road that led out of town. Within minutes they'd passed the campground, which was crowded with everything from pricey recreational vehicles to foldout campers to a few lonely tents that dotted the perimeter of the grounds. She skidded onto the first road to the right and sped down a narrow gravel road leading to the salt marsh that backed up to the campground.

Beside her Brock gripped the edge of the seat and tried to keep from slamming against the door. "This seems like a deserted area. Do you normally patrol down this road?"

"Yes. This has been a hangout for local kids who want to get away from their parents for a while and party. They throw their trash in the salt marsh, and it eventually becomes an environmental hazard. We've also found some underage drinkers down here and even caught a few kids smoking marijuana so we've made this road a part of our patrol. We come down here several times a day."

They turned a corner, and Kate's breath caught in her throat. Doug's squad car sat beside the road, its motor running. The ambulance, its lights blinking, sat beside the cruiser in the road and blocked her view of the scene. The back doors of the ambulance were open. She stopped her car behind Doug's.

A woman and a man she'd never seen before stood at the side of the road. The man had his arm around the woman, and she had her head on his shoulder. They straightened as the squad car pulled to a stop. The woman raised her arm and pointed a trembling finger to the front of the ambulance.

Kate was out of the squad car as soon as she'd turned off the ignition and sprinted between the ambulance and Doug's cruiser. Brock's footsteps thudded behind her.

When she reached the front of the vehicles, she stopped short, her hand pressed to her mouth. Brock bumped her from behind as he plowed into her.

Kate took a step forward and stared at the scene before her. Doug lay sprawled in the middle of the road. Two EMTs bent over him, their bodies shielding her view. One of them glanced over his shoulder. "Hi, Kate."

She could only see Doug's legs, but they weren't moving. "H-how is he, Jimmy?"

Jimmy pursed his lips and shook his head, then turned back to his task. Kate watched for a moment before she took a deep breath and turned around. Retracing her steps, she approached the couple standing beside the road. "Good morning. I'm Deputy Kate Michaels. Are you the ones who made the 911 call?"

The man nodded and pointed in the direction of the campground. "We're staying over at Swanson's, and we've been taking a walk down this road every morning since we've been here. When we saw the officer lying in the road, I called for help."

"Did you see anyone else around?"

"No. He was just lying there. I bent down to see if he was breathing, but I couldn't tell."

"There was so much blood." The man's wife burst into tears.

Kate's stomach roiled at the idea of Doug lying on a deserted road. She swallowed and tried to suppress the tears threatening to flood her eyes. "When you came down the road, did you meet any cars or see any on the main road?"

They both shook their heads. "No."

Brock walked up to Kate and touched her arm. "Kate, the EMTs want to see you a minute. They're getting ready to transport Doug."

She glanced back at the couple. "Please don't leave. I need to get your names and contact information."

She turned, strode back to front of the ambulance and sagged against the fender. Doug's body with a white sheet covering it lay on a gurney. "No," she moaned.

Jimmy walked over and put his hand on her shoulder. "I know how you must feel, Kate. I want you to know we did everything we could, but we couldn't resuscitate him. He was already dead when we got here."

A tear trickled down the side of her face, and she wiped at it. "How did he die?"

Jimmy's brow wrinkled. "Stab wounds. Whoever did this was up close when he attacked Doug." He glanced back at the body. "We'll take him back to the Health Center. You can come by there when you get through here."

She bit her lip and nodded. Jimmy turned back to Doug's body, and within minutes they had him loaded into the ambulance. Kate tried to shake the scene from her head as she took down the information of the couple who'd found Doug's body.

When she'd finished and they had left, she glanced around to see Brock waiting for her beside the squad car. She walked over to him. "Thanks for coming with me."

"I'm glad I was here. I know this was tough for you."

"Yeah." She glanced around. "I want to take a look in Doug's car and see if I can find anything before I go."

"Are you going to lift any fingerprints?"

"I think I'd better. I doubt if the killer left any prints, but I'd rather check it out. My equipment bag is in the trunk."

He put his hand on her arm. "I'll get it. The keys are still in the car. I'll unlock the trunk and bring it to you."

"Thanks, Brock."

Kate waited for Brock to return, then pulled some latex gloves from the bag. After putting them on, she opened the door of the car and looked inside. She gasped aloud, and her body quaked like a jolt of electricity had just surged through her.

An envelope with her name in block letters sat taped to the steering wheel.

"No," she groaned.

Brock leaned over her shoulder to look inside. "It looks like your killer left you a message, Kate."

With shaking fingers, she picked up the envelope and unsealed it. Pulling a sheet of paper out, she unfolded it and read the words printed on the page.

Kate, I'm sorry about your friend. But you know what they say—Only the Good Die Young. I'll Be Seeing You.

Kate stared at the paper in her hand, and a rage like she'd never known coursed through her body. Her instinct told her to crush the paper into a ball and hurl it as far away as possible. Instead she held up the envelope and studied it. Her heartbeat slowed, and her mouth curled into a smile. "Well, well, you may have made your first mistake."

Brock frowned. "What do you mean?"

Kate arched an eyebrow and held up the envelope. "The other two envelopes had no fingerprints, and I doubt if this one will, either. But the others had the flap tucked down inside the envelope. He sealed this one. That means he must have licked it. Now I have his DNA."

She leaned down, pulled a plastic bag from the equipment case and dropped the letter inside. She straightened and stared at Brock. "Doug didn't deserve what happened to him. I don't know who did this to him, but I'm going to find out. And when I do, this piece of evidence will send Doug's killer to prison for the rest of his life."

EIGHT

Brock still hadn't shaken the events of the day from his mind as he guided the car off the main road onto the path that led to the house where Kate and her sisters lived. The headlights of his car cut a swath down the road toward the home that Kate's grandparents had built close to the ocean years before the beaches had been included in the Cape Hatteras National Seashore.

He rounded a corner and pulled to a stop in the yard of the weathered two-story frame house he'd visited so many times in the past. It hadn't changed in the past six years. A shed next to the house served as a garage, and he could see Kate's squad car inside.

The house sat nestled at the end of the road next to the beach dunes, and the sound of the ocean breaking onshore drifted from the other side. A light burned in a downstairs window. Upstairs curtains fluttered at an open window on the breeze blowing off the water.

It had been six years since he'd seen this house, and yet it seemed like it was only yesterday. Perhaps it was the fact that its image had been permanently branded in his mind. It was as much a part of Kate as the island itself.

He stepped from the car, and the crunch underneath his feet made him smile. Oyster shells dotted the sandy soil. That hadn't changed either. The only thing that had changed was why he was here.

Taking a deep breath, he climbed the steps to the front door and knocked. It was opened almost immediately by Emma. Her face broke into a big smile. "Brock," she squealed. She grabbed his arm and pulled him inside, then glanced over her shoulder. "Betsy, Brock is here."

Betsy, holding a dish towel, hurried into the room. A slight frown wrinkled her forehead. "Brock, what are you doing here?"

"I came to see Kate. I thought all of you might be at Treasury's for dinner, but you weren't."

Betsy glanced at Emma and handed her the dish towel. "Emma, will you finish drying the dishes while I talk to Brock?"

Emma's lip protruded in a pout. "But I want to talk to Brock, too."

Betsy smiled and patted her hand. "You can when you finish the dishes. Now run along."

Emma's shoulders drooped as she walked from the room. "Don't leave without telling me, Brock."

He laughed. "I won't."

When Emma was out of earshot, Betsy turned back to him and placed her hands on her hips. "What do you want?" she snapped.

She'd made it evident when she'd seen him at Treasury's that she wasn't happy about his being back on the island. Distrust flickered in her eyes. He didn't flinch from her steady gaze. "I want to talk to Kate."

Betsy arched an eyebrow. "Why?"

He swallowed and took a deep breath. "I was with her at the scene of Doug's murder. I know how upset she was. I just want to make sure she's all right."

Betsy studied him for a moment. "It's taken her a long time

to get over her breakup with you, but she's finally done it. I don't want to see Kate hurt again."

"I don't, either. I promise you that's not my intention. I don't know how much Kate's told you about this case she's working on, but I'm worried for her."

Betsy frowned. "Worried? Why?"

"I think she's got some big problems at work, and I want to help her. I don't want anything to happen to her."

Betsy's eyes grew wide. "Happen to her? Do you think she's in some kind of danger?"

"She could be. You really need to talk to Kate about it, but I think she needs some help on this investigation. I'm a police detective, Betsy. I want to be there if she needs me."

Betsy chewed on her lip as her gaze drifted across his face. After a moment she spoke. "I don't want anything to happen to my sister."

"Neither do I. Now would you please tell her I'm here?"

"She isn't here."

"But her car's in the garage."

"She took a walk after dinner and hasn't come back. She does that a lot. She's probably on the beach somewhere."

Brock smiled. "I know where she is."

He hurried from the house and headed toward the dunes and the beach. Although darkness covered the area, a security light at the edge of the yard lit the path that led up the dune and onto the beach. When he stepped onto the beach, his feet sank into the sand, and he stopped. The light didn't extend this far from the house, and he stood in total darkness.

Moonlight glimmered on the water a hundred yards away, and he eased toward it. He knew Kate would be sitting halfway between the water and the dunes. As he walked forward, he called her name.

"Kate, it's Brock. Where are you?"

"I'm here." Her voice came from directly ahead. A flashlight beam swept over him. "I'll light your way to where I am."

He followed the light to where she sat and then he dropped down beside her. He settled onto the sand, stretched his legs out and leaned back on his arms. She switched off the light, and the black night closed in around them. He closed his eyes for a moment and listened to the waves breaking on the beach. How many times had they sat like this in the past? His heart ached for the loss of what had been between them years ago.

After a moment she spoke. "Can you hear it, Brock?"

Puzzled, he opened his eyes. "What?"

"God's voice."

Her words surprised him, and he turned toward her. In the moonlight her skin seemed to glow in an almost ethereal manner. "What are you talking about?"

A breeze blew off the water and ruffled her hair. She reached up and smoothed it back into place. "When I'm on the beach, He's everywhere around me. I can hear Him, and I know He's with me."

Captivated by her appearance and the huskiness of her voice, Brock leaned toward her. "How do you hear Him?"

She tilted her face to the sky. "Listen to the sounds around you. What do you hear?"

He squinted in concentration and tried to distinguish sounds in the night. "I hear the ocean and the soft moan of the wind." A loud, harsh squawk almost like a small dog barking drifted on the night air. "What was that?"

"A Black-crowned Night Heron. It's their feeding time."

He still didn't understand. He swiveled to face Kate. "Why do you want me to hear these sounds?"

"Because you wanted to find God on this island, and He's here. He's in the music that the wind and waves make and in the calls of the wildlife here. Every day I thank Him for making this beautiful world and for letting me be a part of it."

He listened again. "How do you really know He's here?"

She closed her eyes and lifted her face to the breeze. "How do you know the wind is here?"

"Because I feel it."

"I feel Him. If you'll open your heart, you can feel Him, too."

He tilted his head to the side and exhaled. "You can say that God's here after what happened to Doug today?"

She clasped her hands in front of her and stared at the ocean. "I've been talking with Him about that. I don't understand why Doug had to die. I may never understand that. In our line of work, though, we see bad things happen to good people every day. Understanding is not the point. Helping do something about the bad things in the world is."

"But what if you get hurt in the process?"

She shrugged. "I guess that's a chance we take. The early believers didn't renounce their faith even when it cost them their lives. Their faith is an example to me to keep on believing in God's love even when the bad times come. So, I put my trust in Him and believe that in the end, whatever happens is His will."

His heart thudded. "B-but this killer has threatened you. Do you think God is really going to protect you from being a victim, too?"

"I don't know. I just know I have a peace about this situation. I placed my life in God's hands years ago, and I can face whatever comes my way."

Her soft voice rippled through his mind like the waves washing up on the sand. He wanted to believe like she did, but something held him back. He reached for her hand and covered it with his. To his surprise, she didn't draw back from his touch.

"I hope you're right. But just to make sure, I don't plan to let you out of my sight. What did Sheriff Baxter say when he came to the island this afternoon?"

She glanced down at their clasped hands before she slipped hers free and pushed to her feet. "He was very upset over Doug's death. We only have five deputies on the mainland to cover the rest of the county, and one of them is off sick. They're involved in trying to solve a burglary ring that's operating all over the county. They've stolen thousands of dollars over the past few months."

"Are they targeting homes or businesses?"

"Both, but they seem to like homes better. They're very selective and only take small, expensive items they can conceal and fence easily. But with our deputies working on that case, the department's in a bind. Sheriff Baxter can't send anyone over to help Calvin and me, so the park rangers are going to help out with patrol for now."

"Is that unusual?"

She shook her head. "No. They help us out whenever we need them." She was silent for a moment. "Doc sent over the personal effects that were on Doug's body. The strange thing is that his cell phone was missing."

"What do you think that means?" he asked.

"I have no idea."

"It could have been dropped at the crime scene, and we didn't notice it. Maybe it will turn up tomorrow. Try not to think about it tonight. You've had a rough day." He rose and dusted the sand from the seat of his pants. "While I'm here, I'll volunteer and help out any way I can. Just tell me what to do."

"Thanks, Brock. I appreciate that." She switched the flashlight on. "I think I'd better be getting home. I have an early day tomorrow."

"I'll come to the station in the morning."

She directed the light's beam toward the dunes and started walking. He stayed beside her until they reentered the front yard of the house. Emma sat on the steps with her elbows on her knees and her chin resting in her hands. She jumped to her feet when she saw them.

"Brock," she cried. "I thought you'd never come back."

Emma jumped down the steps and ran toward them. She stopped in front of Kate and smiled up at her. "Can Brock come in and watch TV with us?"

Before Kate could answer, Brock shook his head. "Not tonight, Emma. Your sister is tired, and she probably wouldn't appreciate all our noise. How about if we do it another night?"

Emma gazed up at her sister. "Can he come another night for dinner, Kate? I'll help cook."

Kate frowned. "I don't..." She stopped and glanced at Brock, then to Emma who had her hands clasped under her chin in a pleading manner. With a laugh, Kate smoothed a wayward strand of hair behind Emma's ear. "I suppose he can."

"When?"

Kate's forehead wrinkled. "One night next week after the festival is over."

Emma turned to Brock. "Are you coming to see me in the play?"

He glanced at Kate. "When is it?"

"The festival starts Friday. The play is that night at the Hurricane Theater. Emma is playing a servant girl who works for Blackbeard. This is her first part in a play."

"Then I wouldn't miss the performance." He laughed and chucked Emma under the chin. "I want to be there to witness a rising star."

Emma's eyes grew wide. "A rising star? Do you really think so?"

He nodded. "I know so."

Emma glanced up at Kate. "Then Kate will save you a seat. You can sit with her and Betsy and Treasury. When I look out at the audience, I can see all of you together."

Smiling, Kate put her arm around her sister. "You need to concentrate on saying your line instead of seeing who's looking at you. Now you run on inside. I'll be there in a few minutes." She watched Emma scamper up the steps before she turned back to Brock. "Thanks for coming tonight, and thank you for being with me today."

He shoved his hands in his pockets and balled his fingers into his palms. He wanted to put his arms around her and hold her, but he knew he gave up that privilege years ago. "I'm glad I was there, too. I'll see you tomorrow."

"Have a good night."

She turned and climbed the steps to the porch. He watched until she'd disappeared into the house before he trudged back to his car. *Have a good night.* Her words echoed in his thoughts. It had been so long since he'd had a peaceful night's sleep that he'd almost forgotten what it felt like.

He opened the door of his car and stopped at the squawk he'd heard earlier on the beach. A Black-crowned Night Heron, Kate said. He stood beside the open door of the car and closed his eyes. The bird's call drifted on the wind that blew in his face, and on the other side of the dunes he could hear the waves rolling onshore.

As he listened to the sounds that Kate said told her of God's presence, he blocked everything else from his mind and concentrated. If there was something he'd been missing for years, he wanted to find it. Could it really be that simple? Did he just need to look around at the world and listen to the sounds in it to detect the presence of God?

He opened his eyes and turned to stare at Kate's house. He didn't understand all that she'd tried to tell him tonight about

God and the faith she had, but the memory of her words made the blood rush in his veins. Something told him that tonight he had taken his first step toward finding that elusive peace he wanted.

For the first time in months he felt happy. Even with all the bad things happening around them, his heart felt lighter than it had in months. Maybe it was God, and maybe it was just being around Kate again. Whatever had made it happen, he knew he would sleep well tonight for the first time in a long while.

He held his hands under the hot water and rubbed the bar of soap over his reddened skin. How many times had he scrubbed since he'd been back? Even though he'd worn gloves, he still felt the need to wash his hands again.

He raised his hands in front of his face and stared at them. *So now I've done murder.*

He hadn't been sure he could. Not until the last moment when he plunged the knife into that deputy's back. He didn't want to do it. In fact, he had debated right up until the last minute. In the end, though, he had no choice. Kate had to know he meant business. Now she would be looking over her shoulder every minute, and when she least expected it he would strike.

He dried his hands and hung the towel back on the rack by the sink. He stared at it for a moment before he reached out and adjusted the towel so that it hung evenly over the rung. Nice and tidy, that was the way he liked things. Just like today when he'd pretended to have car trouble.

He knew that deputy, whose name tag said Doug McNeil, would stop and ask if he could help. Kate had trained him well.

He pulled the deputy's cell phone from his pocket, flipped it open and scrolled through the list of contacts until he found

Kate's number. Chuckling, he closed the phone, stuck it back in his pocket, and moved from the bathroom into the bedroom. He stopped to straighten a picture that hung on the wall before he crossed the room to sit in the chair by the window. An edition of the island publication that listed all upcoming events lay on a table beside the chair. He picked it up and began to skim the articles about the weekend festival. It seemed that everybody was gearing up to cater to the crowds that would arrive in a few days.

His eye caught sight of the article about the play *Blackbeard's Last Stand* that would be presented at the Hurricane Theater on Friday and Saturday nights. The caption underneath a picture depicting a scene from the play identified Emma Michaels as the young girl standing beside a wooden table where a group of pirates sat eating.

He pulled the paper closer and studied the girl's features. Kate's little sister would be playing a part in the production. He hadn't expected this opportunity. How could he use this to his advantage?

He folded the paper and laid it on the table beside him. The play was several days away. He had time to plan how he could make Friday night's performance unforgettable.

NINE

On Friday morning Kate pulled the squad car to a stop behind Treasury's bed-and-breakfast, climbed out, and glanced up at the clear sky. The forecast predicted temperatures in the mid-eighties for the day. That should make it perfect weather for the opening of the festival.

It was only seven-thirty, but the local merchants and artists were already setting up booths when she'd driven through the village. She expected a busy day and was glad that Brock was riding patrol with her, as he had every day since Doug's murder.

She bit down on her bottom lip at the thought of the young deputy. She missed him so much. Several times yesterday she'd reached for her cell phone to give Doug a call and then been hit with the cold reality that she would never talk with him again.

It didn't make any sense why the killer would target Doug. She was the one he wanted, not a young man who hoped only to make a difference in this world. His dreams and plans for the future had been cut short. She would never understand what caused some people to have so little regard for human life. Doug didn't deserve what happened to him on that deserted road, and she was determined to bring his killer to justice.

She slammed the door of the car and strode across the backyard. She'd just stepped onto the back porch when the door opened and Dillon McAllister emerged. He smiled when he saw her.

"Hi, Kate. What are you doing here so early?"

"Brock's riding with me on patrol. I came by to get him." She noticed that today he wore jeans and a short-sleeved T-shirt. "Are you off for another day with Grady?"

He laughed. "Yeah. Thanks for introducing me to him. He's been a great help, and I've gotten to see parts of the island that most tourists never see."

Kate cocked an eyebrow. "Just be careful about using the information he gives you. Some of it is pure speculation and other parts are stories that have been passed down in his family."

"I know, but he really does have a grasp of that period of history. Even though he insists that Blackbeard's money tree is out there somewhere, I doubt it. I think you're right about Blackbeard's treasure. All you have to do is study the way this island has shifted and changed in the past two hundred years to realize that anything that was here then is now washed out to sea or at the bottom of a salt marsh."

"Yeah." Before she could add another comment, angry voices blared through the open back door.

"Tracey, will you leave me alone? You know this is my only vacation of the year."

Kate and Dillon glanced at each other. "That's Sam and Tracey," he whispered. "They started fighting at breakfast. It still seems to be going on."

"But why do you have to fish every day? I'm tired of being alone. Why can't you go with me to the beach, or at least let me go on the boat with you? I can work on my tan while you fish." The whine in Tracey's voice reminded Kate of Emma when she didn't get her way. Tracey, however, was an adult, while Emma was still a child.

"We've been over this a hundred times," Sam yelled. "I've tried taking you fishing, and you just get bored. Then you want to go back to shore. I want to fish, and I can't do that with you along."

"You're being mean."

"Mean?" Sam roared. "You're a fine one to talk. Take this money and go shopping today or do whatever you want. Just let me have some peace and quiet for a change. Now I'm off to the marina. I'm going to rent me a boat, and when I come back, I'll take you to the festival tonight."

"But Sam—" Tracey's last words were cut off by Sam's hurried exit through the back door.

Sam stepped onto the back porch and halted as he came face-to-face with Kate and Dillon. His face turned crimson, and he gave a nervous laugh. "I'm afraid my wife is a little upset this morning. Sorry about that."

Kate tried to breathe, but she felt as if she'd been kicked in the stomach. It wasn't the argument she'd just heard or Sam's obvious embarrassment that shocked her into silence. It was what he was wearing—a hooded sweatshirt. The memory of a fishing skiff captained by a lone figure in a hooded sweatshirt returned. That person had also made an ominous promise that he would be seeing her. Had Doug's killer been this close to her all along? She tried to respond, but her vocal chords felt frozen.

Dillon glanced at her, frowned, and turned to Sam. "Have a good day on the water. Maybe we can get together at the festival tonight."

"Okay." Sam glanced at Kate once more before he ducked his head, walked past them, and hurried down the steps.

Kate's stomach roiled and her pulse raced at the sight of Sam's retreating figure. She didn't move until he disappeared around the side of the house toward the area where Treasury's guests parked their cars.

Dillon stepped closer to her. "What's the matter, Kate? You look like you've seen a ghost."

She pulled her attention back to Dillon. "It's nothing. I was just looking at that sweatshirt Sam was wearing. It seems strange that he would wear a sweatshirt to go fishing."

Dillon nodded. "Yeah. I wondered that, too. It's going to get hotter as the day goes on." He glanced at his watch and gasped. "I've got to get going. Grady is going to wonder what happened to me."

"Have a good day. I'll see you at the festival tonight."

With a wave Dillon disappeared in the same direction that Sam had gone. After a moment Kate turned and walked into the kitchen. Treasury stood at the sink but looked up when Kate entered.

Kate walked over and put her arms around Treasury's shoulders. "Good morning, Treasury. I'm here to pick up Brock. Do you know where he is?"

"Morning, darling." She arched her eyebrows and nodded toward the dining room. "He's in there."

The sound of muffled crying came from inside. Kate frowned and walked to the dining-room door. The soft tone of Brock's voice kept her from entering.

"I'm sure Sam will be as sorry about your argument as you are. Now you need to dry those tears and decide what you're going to do to occupy yourself today."

"But it's no fun doing something by yourself." The whine of Tracey's voice set Kate's teeth on edge. It reminded her of how Jake Morgan used to scratch his fingernails down the blackboard at school when the teacher was out of the room.

Brock chuckled. "Go on out to the beach. I'm sure you won't be alone for long."

"Why don't you go with me? We could have a good time together."

The whine of Tracey's voice had softened into a purr like a kitten. Kate sucked in her breath and waited for Brock's answer.

"I can't, Tracey. I'm waiting for Kate so I can go on patrol with her. I'm sure you'll be fine."

"Why do you want to ride around in an old police car all day when you could be lying on the beach in the sun?"

Brock laughed. "I'd probably get sunburned, but you go on and have a good time."

"But Brock..."

Kate had heard enough. She stepped into the room. Tracey and Brock sat at the dining-room table. Brock's arm rested on the table. Tracey's fingers trailed up the back of his hand and stopped above his wrist. Her eyelids drooped, and her mouth curled into a smile as her hand tightened.

Kate coughed, and they jerked their attention to her. She looked from one to the other and smiled. "Good morning. Are you ready to go, Brock?"

Tracey's face hardened into a stare, but Brock pulled free of Tracey and jumped to his feet. "I am." He pushed his chair in and hurried around the table toward her. "Tracey offered to keep me company while I was waiting."

"It's good to see you again, Tracey. I hope you enjoy your day on the island. Everybody is getting ready for the festival tonight, so there ought to be a lot of activity around today."

"So I've heard." Anger flickered in Tracey's eyes. She gave a curt nod and pushed to her feet. "Thanks."

Kate watched Tracey hurry from the room before she followed Brock into the kitchen and stopped beside Treasury at the sink. "Don't forget we're going to see Emma in the play tonight."

"I haven't forgotten, but you remember to be careful today."

Treasury dried her hands on a towel before she cast a worried look in Brock's direction. "I feel better knowing that Brock's with you, but both of you take care. There's a killer out there, and I don't want anyone I love to be hurt."

Kate reached over and gave Treasury a peck on the cheek. "I will be careful. See you later."

She walked out the back door with Brock on her heels, but she stopped on the back porch and turned to him. "Brock, you don't have to go with me if there's something else you'd rather do today."

A puzzled expression covered his face. "I've gone with you every morning for the past three days. Why would you think I wouldn't want to go today?"

She nodded toward the house. "I heard Tracey asking you to go to the beach with her. You haven't had time to relax since you've been here. If you'd rather go with her, I'll understand."

His eyes grew wide, and his mouth dropped open. After a moment he shook his head. "Sam and Tracey started arguing at breakfast this morning, then they took it to their room. We could hear them downstairs. After he left, she came in the dining room crying. I was trying to comfort her when you came in. That's all it was."

She looked down at the key ring in her hand as if she'd never seen it before. Her face burned from his scrutiny, but she avoided meeting his gaze. "It sounded like it was more than that."

The sound of his loud gasp caused her to glance up. With teeth gritted, he took a step toward her. "What's that supposed to mean?"

She shrugged. "Just that Tracey's a very attractive woman. I wouldn't blame you for wanting to spend the day with her instead of in *an old police car*." She tried to mimic the sound Tracey had made when she spoke those words.

He exhaled and shook his head. "Tracey is a *married* woman. I didn't realize that your opinion of me was so low that you'd think I could be interested in a married woman."

The hurt in his eyes pricked her heart, but of more concern was the fact that she had spoken without thinking. She struggled to say something that would ease the sting of her words. "I just thought—"

He held up a hand to stop her. "Don't bother explaining. I understand." He sidestepped her and started down the steps toward the car. "Come on. It's time we started patrol."

Kate stood on the back porch, her heart pounding in her chest. What was wrong with her? She knew in her heart that Brock would never do what she had accused him of. And yet, the words she'd used held a not-so-subtle meaning that she didn't trust him. Why had she done that?

The truth hit her, and her mind reeled from the impact. When she'd heard Tracey flirting with Brock, she'd been jealous. She had ignored Brock's responses and concentrated on Tracey's words. In so doing, she had allowed a long-buried feeling for him to emerge, and she had reacted as she might have done six years ago. She had to make sure that didn't happen again.

Since Brock had been on the island, they had been finding their way to a new relationship—a friendship that would take the place of what they'd once had. Now she was trying to come to grips with the past and forgive him for hurting her, but it was so hard.

Her words had hurt Brock, and she was sorry for that. She would find some way today to ask his forgiveness. But if she couldn't forgive him, why did she think he would forgive her? Maybe it would be best if she and Brock didn't discuss personal matters but instead concentrated on finding the killer who was stalking her.

* * *

Brock sighed and glanced at his watch as Kate pulled the squad car to a stop in front of the police station. Five o'clock. It had been a long and trying day. The chill inside the car hadn't been caused by the air conditioner. It came directly from the frosty responses he'd gotten every time he tried to engage Kate in conversation. She had given so many one-syllable answers that he finally gave up even trying to talk with her.

Thankfully, there hadn't been any problems or emergencies. In fact all the people he'd encountered had been in a festive mood as they'd prepared for the opening of the festival tonight. He thought back over the islanders he'd met. Some he remembered. Others were new to Ocracoke. They'd all been so excited about the upcoming festivities. It would have been easy to get swept up in the excitement if it hadn't been for the silent treatment he'd gotten from Kate since they left the bed-and-breakfast that morning.

Beside him, she opened the door and glanced at him. "Are you coming inside?"

He looked at her and tried to see a sign that she wanted him to go with her, but her face held a blank expression. He sighed and shook his head. "I don't think so. I promised Will Scott I'd come back by his booth to help him unload the pottery he's bringing from his studio. I'll walk back to Treasury's house after we get his booth set up."

"Are you coming to the festival tonight?"

He reached for the handle and opened the door. "I promised Emma I'd come to see her performance. I'll be there."

"The Hurricane Theater is an open-air area. There aren't any seats. We'll bring a lawn chair for you. Emma wants you to sit with us."

He bit his lip. Emma, not Kate, and certainly not Betsy,

wanted him to sit with them. He wondered how Treasury felt about him. He sighed and stepped from the car. When he turned back to close the door, she was standing next to the driver's side, staring at him over the top of the car.

Even after a day of patrol and being in and out of the heat, she looked as fresh as the morning glories that used to bloom outside his window when he was a boy. Her face glowed in the late afternoon sun, and he was struck once again with how beautiful she was. A longing for what had been between them flowed through him, and he slammed the car door with a force that almost rattled the windows.

"I'll see you at the theater," he mumbled, and turned away.

He shoved his hands in his pockets and strode down the street without a backward glance. A longing for his apartment in Nashville overtook him, and he wished he was there. He could go home if he wanted to. It didn't look as if his trip to Ocracoke was going to produce what he'd hoped.

Kate was never going to forgive him or trust him again. And the peace that her mother spoke of was still as much a mystery to him as it had been six years ago. He'd go to the play tonight, then tomorrow he'd go home and try to deal with his guilt as best he could.

He stopped without warning in the middle of the sidewalk and pressed his palm to his forehead. What was he thinking? He couldn't go home. He'd promised Kate that he would be there for her until this killer was caught. If he left and something happened to her, he'd never be able to forgive himself.

Maybe they would catch this killer soon. Every day he stayed here brought back too many reminders of the past. And those memories were beginning to break through the barrier he had put around his heart. He couldn't let Kate see what was happening to him because she would distance herself from him forever, and he doubted he could survive losing her a second time. But one thing was for sure. As soon as they found Doug's killer, he was getting off this island.

TEN

Kate watched Brock walk away from the police station. She'd tried to apologize several times today for her behavior this morning, but each time the words stuck in her throat. He'd been quiet all day, and she hadn't pushed him to talk.

It was probably best. No good could come from their becoming friends again. She had to keep remembering how hard it had been to get over him. She didn't want to go through that again, and she would if she didn't watch out. Brock might seem different than he was when they were younger, but underneath he was still the same. And he would leave again just like he had six years ago.

With a sigh she pulled her attention away from Brock's retreating figure and trudged up the steps of the police station. An empty office greeted her. Lisa, always eager to hear about what she'd encountered when she returned from patrol, wasn't behind her desk. A sob came from the break room behind the dispatch area.

Kate hurried across the outer office and stared into the room that contained a couch, chairs and a small table with a coffeepot on it. Lisa lay facedown on the couch, her body shaking with sobs. Kate rushed to her and knelt beside the sofa.

"Lisa, what's wrong? Are you sick?"

A soft wail escaped Lisa's mouth, and she buried her head in her folded arms. She shook her head. "N-no."

Kate placed her hand on the back of Lisa's head and stroked her hair. "Tell me what's happened. I want to help you."

Lisa pushed up into a sitting position and pulled a tissue from her pocket. She dabbed at the tears that streamed from her eyes. "I—I'm s-sorry. I just needed to take a break. I'll get back to my desk."

Lisa started to rise, but Kate put her hand on her arm. "Please, Lisa. Tell me what's bothering you."

Tears welled in Lisa's eyes again. "It's Doug. I can't believe he's gone."

Kate pushed up from her knees, dropped onto the couch next to Lisa and rubbed her hand across her eyes. "I know. I can't believe it, either. I keep expecting him to walk in the door with that crooked smile on his face."

With a sob Lisa dissolved into tears again. Kate put her arm around the girl's shaking shoulders and pulled her closer. The memory of Doug's body lying in the road returned, and she squeezed her eyes shut to blot out the image, but it did no good. That scene was still too vivid in her mind, and she doubted if it would dim soon.

They didn't speak as the tears rolled down their faces. After a few minutes Lisa raised her head, straightened her back and pounded her fists on her knees. "I was so awful to Doug. I'll never be able to forgive myself for the way I treated him."

Kate stared at her in amazement. "How can you say that? Doug liked you a lot."

"I know. He kept asking me to go out with him, but I'd always have some excuse. The real reason was that the only person I wanted was Calvin. I kept telling myself that he was going to ask me out, but I think I knew that wasn't true.

Calvin loves the attention he gets from women. He flirts with every woman who comes in here."

"I think you're right about Calvin. He seems to attract women wherever he goes."

Lisa snorted. "Yeah, and I thought he'd settle for me. But lately I've thought he might be seeing someone on the mainland."

The statement surprised Kate. She'd never heard Calvin mention anyone special. "What makes you think so?"

Lisa shrugged. "He's been spending his weekends off on the mainland. He's never said anything, but I've seen him boarding the ferry in the late afternoons a lot lately."

Kate pursed her lips and tried to remember Calvin mentioning going to the mainland. "I didn't know that. He never said anything. So you think he went to spend time with a woman?"

"Yeah. One day I overheard him on his cell phone, and he was talking to someone about meeting that night at Lakeview Lodge. He said he was expecting a really good time. I kept hoping he'd notice how crazy I was about him. And all that time there was Doug, a nice guy who wanted to get to know me better, and I wouldn't give him the time of day. Now it's too late."

Kate chewed on her lip and nodded. Lisa's words brought to mind how she'd felt since Brock came to the island. He said he wanted to find peace and to be her friend, but she hadn't been willing to meet him halfway. Maybe tonight she would have an opportunity to apologize to him for her behavior today. He didn't have to volunteer his time to help out the department, and she needed to remember that.

Lisa pushed to her feet. "I need to get back to work." She walked to the door but stopped and turned back to face Kate. "Oh, I have some messages for you. One from Sheriff Baxter. He called this afternoon."

Kate followed Lisa into the outer office and stopped beside the dispatch desk. "I was hoping we'd hear from him. Did he have any news about fingerprints or DNA from the envelope in Doug's car?"

"No, he said the lab in Raleigh is backed up and won't have the results for some time. He wanted to let us know that there haven't been any new leads in the burglary ring that's operating on the mainland. The last robbery occurred last week at a home in Swan Quarter. The method of entry was the same. The occupants were gone overnight, so the thieves had time to completely go through the house. They even opened a safe and took a lot of jewelry from it."

"That sounds like they knew what they were looking for. Did Sheriff Baxter give you a description of any of the jewelry?"

"Yes. He wanted you and Calvin to be on the lookout for any items that might find their way into the pawn shop here." Lisa picked up a stack of papers from her desk. "He faxed these pictures to us. The lady whose house was burglarized had insured her jewelry, and she had pictures of all her pieces."

Kate flipped through the papers. Pictures of jewelry, cameras and assorted video equipment filled the pages. She gave a low whistle at one photograph. "Look at this bracelet. The description says it has one hundred sixty-seven diamonds and twenty emeralds on it. The diamonds and the emeralds each have a seven-carat weight. It says this bracelet is valued at over twenty-five thousand dollars." She glanced up at Lisa. "How would you like to wear that on your arm?"

"Not me. I'd be scared I'd lose it. Sheriff Baxter said the owner was really upset over that bracelet. It's been in her family for nearly two hundred years. She was thinking of putting it up for auction at Christie's in New York, but she hadn't been able to part with it."

Kate laid the pictures down. "Well, the owner has lost it now. Maybe we'll get lucky and it'll turn up somewhere. This burglary ring is about to drive Sheriff Baxter crazy."

"Why does he think it's a ring?"

"There has to be more than one person because in the past there have been two robberies at the same time, but they'd be miles apart in the county. Our deputies are all over the place trying to catch these guys. It sounds like this time it might have taken more than one robber if the house was searched as thoroughly as it seems." She shook her head. "I sure hope these guys don't show up on Ocracoke. We've got enough to contend with right now without adding burglary."

The front door opened, and they both turned as Calvin entered. He flashed a smile in their direction. "I expected to see you two dressed like pirates. The tourists are already beginning to show up for the festival, and they're decked out in some cool costumes." He stopped beside Lisa's desk and let his gaze travel over her face. "What about you? Do you have your outfit for tonight?"

Lisa glanced at Kate and bit down on her lip before she answered. "I'm wearing the same one I did last year." She handed Calvin the stack of pictures. "I know you're about to go on duty, and I don't want to detain you. But you'd better look at these pictures before you do. Sheriff Baxter wants you to keep a lookout for any of these items that might show up at the pawn shop here."

Calvin flipped through the pictures, then laid them on her desk. "I'm going to be patrolling the festival area tonight. Maybe I'll see you there."

Lisa shook her head. "I doubt it. I'm going to see Emma in the play. Then I plan to go right home." She glanced down at her desk and picked up a memo. "One other thing I didn't tell you, Kate. Sheriff Baxter spoke with Clay Phillips about backing up Calvin on patrol tonight. He'll be there from six o'clock until the booths close."

Calvin shrugged. "I doubt if I'll need him. The only problems we ever have at the festival are caused by tourists who have had too much to drink over at the Blue Pelican." He turned to Kate. "Anything else you need to tell me before I take over?"

"Make sure you keep in touch with Clay, and call if you need him. I'll have my cell phone, too." Kate turned to Lisa. "Before you leave, make sure that you route the local calls as well as the 911 emergencies from the mainland terminal to my cell phone for the night."

Lisa nodded. "I will."

"And Calvin, I'll relay anything to you. Do you have any questions?"

"No, it'll just be business as usual. Have a good time, and tell Emma I'll try to get over to the theater to see her. But I may be too busy."

Kate headed to the door. "I'll tell her. And Lisa, we'll save a spot for your lawn chair at the play."

When Kate stepped onto the street, she could hardly believe the number of people who had already arrived for the opening of the festival. She was about to get in her squad car when Emma's voice rang out above the crowd. "Kate, wait."

Emma ran down the sidewalk toward her. Kate smiled as Emma came to a stop in front of her. "What are you doing here? I thought you and Betsy were going to wait for me at home."

"Betsy is over at the booth she and Will Scott are sharing. He picked us up so he could load Betsy's paintings in his van. Brock's over there now helping them put Will's pottery and Betsy's paintings out." She grabbed Kate by the hand. "Come and see."

The mention of Brock sent a guilty reminder of what their

day had been like. She didn't want to see him now. Kate pulled away from Emma and shook her head. "I need to go home and change clothes. I'll be back for the play, though. Tell Betsy I'll bring the lawn chairs."

"Okay."

Kate stared after Emma as she rounded the corner onto the street where the artists had set up their booths. Brock had told her he was going to help Will with his booth, so she shouldn't have been surprised that he was also assisting Betsy. Perhaps *surprised* wasn't the right word.

Ever since Brock had come back, he'd made an effort to make her sisters like him. He'd charmed Emma right off by telling her about her mother. His connection to the mother that she barely remembered had made him a hero of sorts in Emma's eyes.

Then he had made Betsy believe he was only concerned about Kate's safety. Now he was helping her set up her booth. If his intention was to trick her into forgiving him by making allies of her sisters, it wasn't going to work.

If she didn't watch out, he would have them begging her to forgive him, and she wasn't about to let that happen. She had taken care of Betsy and Emma since their mother's death, and she had protected the island residents from those who broke the law. She didn't need Brock Gentry's assistance in either job. After the play tonight, she would tell him she didn't think they needed to spend time together anymore. It was becoming too uncomfortable for her.

It would be best if he would go back to Nashville and deal with his past choices as best he could. If he wasn't around anymore, maybe she could get her life back to normal.

At ten minutes before seven o'clock, Brock stopped at the rear of the Hurricane Theater and let his gaze drift over the outdoor performance area where tourists were treated to musical and theater entertainment all summer. Tonight it looked as if half the visitors to the island had chosen to come see *Blackbeard's Last Stand*.

Lawn chairs dotted the grassy area in front of a wooden platform stage that rose about two feet off the ground. Large hurricane lamps with a candle in each sat at the four corners of the stage, and curtains hanging on a wire across the back of the stage provided a backdrop. A primitive table and crudely fashioned wooden chairs sat in the middle of the stage to give the impression of what an island home might have looked like in the early 1700s.

Brock stood on tiptoe and searched the crowd for Kate. He caught sight of her sitting in a lawn chair in the front row. Lisa sat on one side of her and Betsy on the other. To Betsy's right he could see Treasury with an empty chair beside her. He shook his head in disbelief. Kate had positioned him as far from her as she could.

Pasting a smile on his face, he sidestepped the occupied chairs scattered about until he arrived next to Treasury. He dropped into the empty seat and laughed. "I didn't know if I would make it through the crowd or not."

Treasury reached over and patted his arm. "You're right on time. The play should start any minute."

He leaned forward and stared toward Kate, but she appeared not to notice his presence. After a moment he settled back in the chair and waited for the actors to take their places. The day that had started so badly hadn't gotten any better. He needed to do something about that. He would find the right time after the play was over.

Out of the corner of her eye Kate saw Brock sit down next to Treasury and lean forward to stare at her. She kept her attention directed to what Betsy was saying and didn't look at him. When Lisa talked about Doug earlier, Kate had almost decided to ask Brock to forgive her attitude today. Now that she'd had time to think about it, she knew she couldn't. It would be best for everybody if he left the island. She would tell him that after the performance.

A cymbal clanged backstage, and one of the actors stepped through the center opening in the curtains to the middle of the stage. "Avast, ye landlubbers," he called out. "And welcome to the home of Edward Teach, better known 'round these here parts as Blackbeard the Pirate. 'Twas November 22, 1718, that Blackbeard sailed out t' battle the ships of Lieutenant Robert Maynard and met his doom off the shores o' Ocracoke. Tonight we fly the Jolly Roger again as we take you aft to that moment in history."

He bowed and made a flourish with his hands as the actors filed onstage and took their places. For the next thirty minutes Kate didn't take her eyes off the action occurring in front of her. Her heart swelled with pride when the pirates settled at the table for a meal and called for the serving girl to bring their drinks.

Emma, wearing the long burlap dress Treasury had made, entered carrying a tray filled with large tankards. She moved to the table, served each man, then curtsied before stepping back to stand like an obedient servant girl awaiting further orders from her master.

Kate and Betsy glanced at each other and smiled. Pride lit Betsy's eyes, and Kate was sure it mirrored hers. She was about to lean over and whisper to Betsy when her cell phone chimed, alerting her to a received text message.

She pulled the phone from her pocket and held it as she waited for the moment in the play she'd come to see. Onstage Emma stepped back up to the table and held the pitcher up. "More ale, sir?" she said. Kate mouthed the words with her.

Smiling, she glanced down at her phone. Her thrill over Emma's perfectly delivered line turned to horror. She gasped and grabbed the arm of her chair. The displayed sender's name glowed on the lit screen like hot coals and sent a searing pain to her head. *Doug?* The message had been sent from Doug's phone?

She shook her head. What kind of evil trick was someone playing on her? She clicked on the message, blinked and reread it.

It's showtime, Kate. Watch out for Great Balls of Fire.

Kate swiveled in her chair and scanned the audience for movement. A flash of red to her left caught her attention, and she half-rose to get a better look. A man dressed in a pirate costume and holding a small bag stood to the left side of the stage. A beard and mustache hid his face. A tricorn hat covered his head. He smiled, held up a cell phone and slipped it into his pocket.

Her heart pounded in her ears, and she gulped a big breath into her burning lungs as she pushed to her feet. Before she could take a step, he pulled a bottle with a rag stuffed into the top from the bag. Dropping the bag, he flicked a cigarette lighter on and held the flame up for her to see.

Her eyes widened in understanding. He had a firebomb. She reached for her gun before she remembered that she always left it in her car trunk when she was out of uniform. Gritting her teeth, she charged toward the pirate at the moment he hurled the bottle with the now-burning rag to the stage. She was too late.

The audience screamed as the bottle shattered, sending its deadly cargo of fire dancing across the stage. The pirate saluted her, then turned and ran from the scene. Kate tried to pursue, but panicked playgoers mobbed the exits in an effort to escape the spreading blaze and blocked her way.

"Police! Let me through," Kate yelled. Emma's scream

from the stage stopped her, and she turned to stare at her sister. Her heart leaped to her throat at the sight of her little sister fighting the flames that climbed up the burlap dress. Emma screamed again and turned to run.

"Emma," Kate yelled over the crowd. "Don't run."

She pushed back through the crowd and lunged to the front of the stage. Two actors jumped to the ground blocking her way. She pushed the frightened men aside and fought to get onto the platform. To her right a figure leaped onto the stage, and she recognized Brock.

"Emma," he yelled.

Kate jumped onto the stage, but Brock was in front of her. Avoiding the flames licking at his legs, he vaulted across the stage and grabbed Emma around the waist. He dived off the stage to the ground, covered her with his body and rolled back and forth to extinguish the flames. As Kate dropped down beside them, several actors ran from behind stage with fire extinguishers and doused the fire that now licked at the curtains.

Betsy, Treasury and Lisa rushed to where Kate hovered over Brock and Emma. Betsy dropped to her knees beside Kate. "I-is she all right?"

Brock raised his head and rolled off Emma. Scorch marks and holes where the fabric had burned away covered the front of his shirt. His sleeve hung in blackened tatters. Underneath red splotches of skin stood as a testimony to the agony he'd endured.

Kate's gaze raked Emma from head to toe to determine if she'd been injured. Several burns on her legs appeared to be minor, and Kate pulled Emma into her arms. "Are you all right?"

Tears streamed down the child's face. "My legs hurt some, but I was so scared, Kate." She glanced at Brock, and her chin quivered. "Thank you for saving me, Brock."

Wincing, Brock pushed to his feet and grinned. "I'm glad I was here to help."

Betsy reached for Emma, and Kate stood. The muscle in Brock's jaw twitched, and his eyes appeared dull. Kate had seen that expression once before when he'd suffered a knee injury at a college track meet. Now, he didn't want them to know how much pain he was in from the burns he'd sustained. She reached for his hand and pulled his arm closer to examine it. "Those are some bad burns."

He shook his head and pulled his hand away. "I'm all right. We have to find the guy that did this."

Her eyes grew wide, and she gasped. "I was so scared that I forgot I'm a police officer. I have to alert Calvin."

Pulling her cell phone from her pocket, she punched in Calvin's number. When she completed her call, she turned back to Betsy. "Calvin and Clay will be on the lookout for a pirate in a red costume wearing a tricorn hat, but there are probably dozens dressed like that tonight. I need to join the search. You take Emma and Brock to the Health Center and get their burns treated."

Brock shook his head. "I'm okay. I want to help you look for this guy."

"You're hurt, Brock, and I want you to get some medical attention. If you've already left the Center when I get through, I'll come by Treasury's house. We need to talk."

He swallowed and stared into her eyes. "I think you're right."

Kate tried to smile. "Thank you for saving my sister. I'll see you later."

She turned and ran from the stage. There was nothing she wanted more than to go to the Medical Center with Emma and Brock. But Emma had Betsy and Treasury to take care of her, and Brock would be all right. The important thing was they had agreed to talk.

Now she didn't think she could carry through on her resolve to tell him to leave Ocracoke. When Brock had jumped on that stage to save Emma, she realized she had never really banished him from her heart. The problem was she didn't know what to do about it.

ELEVEN

An hour later Kate and Calvin met in front of the funnel cake vendor's stand. Kate propped her hands on her hips and shook her head. "I don't understand it. He disappeared into thin air. There was so much panic backstage no one saw which way he ran, and nobody on the streets saw a pirate running away from the theater."

Calvin pulled off his hat and mopped at his forehead. "I know. I've talked to a lot of pirates dressed in red in the past hour, but all of them have alibis for where they were. And none of them fit the physical description you gave me."

Kate pursed her lips. "All I could tell you was his height and weight, and he has Doug's cell phone. I don't have any idea what color his hair or eyes were, and I couldn't see his face for the beard and mustache."

"That's because you were so frightened for Emma. Have you talked to Betsy? How is Emma?"

"The burns on her legs are minor, thanks to Brock. I'm afraid he didn't fare as well, though. He had some second-degree burns up his arms and some on his stomach. Doc Hunter says there won't be any permanent scarring, but he said Brock would be in pain for a few days."

Calvin shook his head. "I can't imagine that guy wanting

to hurt Emma. When I see Brock, I'm going to have to thank him for saving her."

The memory of seeing the flames climbing up Emma's dress sent tears to Kate's eyes. "Yeah, I have a lot to thank him for, too." She blinked and glanced around. "Where is Clay?"

Calvin shrugged. "You tell me. I tried and tried to call his cell phone, but he didn't respond. I thought he was supposed to be helping me with patrol tonight."

"He is." Kate clenched her fists and frowned. Where could Clay be? With so many people on the streets tonight, they needed the presence of uniformed figures around.

Calvin pointed down the street and chuckled. "Here he comes now. It's plain to see why we couldn't find him."

Kate glanced in the direction Calvin indicated. Clay, his gaze locked on the young woman walking beside him, held a spool of pink cotton candy in one hand. The young woman wore a long skirt that was gathered at the waist and a peasant-style blouse that made her look as if she'd stepped out of the pages of a pirate story. They stopped in the middle of the side-walk, and Clay popped a bite of the sugary confection into the woman's mouth. They laughed before they turned and walked toward Kate and Calvin.

Kate propped her hands on her hips and scowled. What was he thinking? He was supposed to be on patrol, not out on a date. Clay spotted her, and his step faltered before he took the young woman by the arm and pulled her to where Kate stood.

"Hi, Kate, Calvin," he said. "This is Amber. She's visiting the island from St. Louis."

Kate swallowed back the retort that rose in her throat. She'd always been courteous to tourists, and she wouldn't let her irritation with Clay change that. She smiled and turned to Amber. "I'm Kate Michaels, deputy sheriff on Ocracoke. I hope you're enjoying our festival."

Amber smiled at Kate and tilted her head to one side. Her long, blond hair brushed her shoulders as she gazed up at Clay. "I am now. I just met Clay at the cotton candy booth, and he's been telling me all about your island. There's a lot of history here. He's going to give me a private tour of the lighthouse tonight."

Kate arched her eyebrows and shot a questioning glance at Clay. "Then I hope you're used to staying up late because Clay doesn't get off patrol until all the vendors have closed down." She turned to Calvin. "What time was it last year when the last one left?"

"Not until about one-thirty. None of the artists wanted to leave their work out in the open. It took forever to get everything stored inside."

Amber frowned. "One-thirty? Maybe we'd better plan for tomorrow."

The cotton candy's spool crunched in Clay's hands. His eyes shot sparks at Kate. "No, we'll do it tonight. I was under the impression I worked for the National Park Service, not the Hyde County Sheriff's Department."

Kate smiled at Amber. "Excuse us for a moment. While I'm talking with Clay, I'm sure Calvin will be glad to tell you more about our island history." She took Clay by the arm and pulled him aside. When they were out of earshot, Kate unleashed her fury on Clay. "Let me tell you something," she hissed. "For as long as Ocracoke has been a part of the Hatteras National Seashore, the park rangers here have backed up the deputies when needed. Your supervisor agreed to your assignment tonight, and he isn't going to be happy when Sheriff Baxter calls him tomorrow with the report I'm about to file."

"What's the big deal, Kate? I've been doing patrol like I

was supposed to. Are you jealous because another woman seems to like me?"

Kate couldn't believe her ears. Jealous? Her mouth dropped open. "Have you been in outer space, Clay? Everybody up and down the street is talking about the crazy guy who threw a firebomb on the stage at the Hurricane Theater tonight. We needed you to help us search for him, but you weren't answering your cell phone." She glanced back at Amber. "It's plain to see now why not."

Clay's expression changed from anger to surprise. He pulled his cell phone from his pocket and stared at it before he exhaled. "I didn't realize it was turned off. I'm sorry, Kate, but I haven't heard anything about the fire. Was anybody hurt?"

"No, but it could have been bad."

Clay rubbed his hands over his eyes and groaned. After a moment he took a deep breath and stared into Kate's eyes. "I was having such a good time at the festival I guess I lost sight of why I was here. I let you down tonight, but it won't happen again."

"I hope not."

"I'll tell Amber to go on back to her hotel. Maybe I can see her tomorrow."

Kate's eyes narrowed, and she studied Clay as he trudged back toward Amber. With the fire being the big topic of conversation everywhere she'd been in the past hour, she found it difficult to believe that Clay could be as oblivious to the situation as he professed. And why would he turn off his phone when he knew he might be called at any time to help with an emergency?

Another thought popped into Kate's head. There was still the unanswered question about who left the note in her car the day she was at the beach. Clay had been nearby when that incident occurred, too. Brock had thought that suspicious, but she had been hesitant to think Clay capable of doing anything to hurt her.

When she added the incident of the note to their failure to reach him tonight during the fire, it made her wonder if Clay could be involved in the bizarre acts that had happened in the past week. She had been in law enforcement long enough to know that people could turn out to be completely the opposite of what you thought. After all, she really knew very little about Clay Phillips—only what he'd told her. With that in mind, she would keep an eye on him.

She waited until Amber had left before she rejoined Calvin and Clay. "Okay, let's see where we are with this situation. No one has seen the guy we're looking for. So he's probably left the area and is back wherever he's staying. Maybe we'll get lucky and someone will call in, but we can't count on that. You two continue with your patrol until the vendors have shut down, then Calvin can probably finish the night out."

Calvin nodded. "No problem."

"I'll relieve you in the morning. We're expecting the truck delivering the fireworks for tomorrow night's display on the afternoon ferry, and I'll show the drivers where the crew will set up. Calvin can relieve me at the regular shift change time." She glanced at Clay. "We'll use the other ranger tomorrow night. There's no need for you to pull another night shift."

Clay shrugged. "Suits me."

She glanced from one to the other. "Any questions?" When they both shook their heads, she smiled. "Good. I'm going to the Health Center to check on Emma."

Kate turned and walked away before they could question her more. She hadn't said that she wanted to check on Brock, too, but that had been uppermost in her mind. Emma was fine, but Brock had endured a lot of pain to protect her sister. He needed to be thanked.

She'd only taken a few steps when she heard her name

called. She glanced over her shoulder and caught sight of Sam and Tracey Burnett along with Dillon McAllister hurrying toward her. All three wore costumes she'd seen displayed in the window at the Sun Shop. Tracey held up the hem of her long black-and-white-striped skirt as she tried to keep up with Sam, dressed as Jack Sparrow, and Dillon, dressed as Captain Hook.

Dillon was the first to reach Kate. "We were over at the booth where Betsy's paintings are, and the man there said she was at the Health Center with her little sister. What happened?"

All three listened as she told them of the events of the night. When she finished, she looked from one to another. "Did you see a pirate dressed like I described anywhere tonight?"

They glanced at each other and shook their heads. "Where are you going now, Kate?" Dillon asked.

"I'm going back to the theater to look around once more. Maybe I can find somebody there who remembers seeing something." She glanced at her watch. "When I talked to Betsy, she said she was taking Emma home, and Brock was going to Treasury's. I'll go check on him, then I need to get home. I have patrol early in the morning."

Sam ran his finger around the collar of his shirt. "I'm about ready to get back to the bed-and-breakfast, too. I want to get out on the water early tomorrow morning."

Tracey glared at him. "You just got here. I had to come by myself again like always, and I'm not ready to leave yet."

Dillon glanced at Kate and arched his eyebrows. Before Sam and Tracey could launch into another of their arguments, Kate backed away. "I need to be on my way. Enjoy the night, and I'll see all of you tomorrow."

Dillon nodded. "Tell Brock and Emma we hope they're all right."

"I'll do it." Kate turned and hurried down the street.

When she reached the theater, she walked through the gate into the open area where earlier people had sat in lawn chairs and laughed and visited with those seated near them. Now trash littered the area left by those who had sipped sodas and eaten sandwiches as they awaited the beginning of the play.

She walked to the deserted stage, and her stomach roiled at the burned marks across its surface. The singed curtains still hung from the wire across the backdrop, and she closed her eyes for a moment as she recalled the terror of seeing Emma's dress in flames.

She'd promised her mother she would always protect Emma, but tonight that hadn't been possible. What would she have done if Brock hadn't been there? The thought of her little sister dead or scarred for life from the burns made her nauseous, and she sat down on the edge of the stage.

Only a few nights ago she'd told Brock that she had faith God would take care of her. She'd wanted him to understand that she didn't fear death because He would be there with her. Tonight her life hadn't been threatened. Her sister had been the target, and that made her question how strong her faith really was. How could God let a child be hurt?

She closed her eyes and wrestled with the question that repeated in her mind. After a moment she stood and stared up at the sky. She believed that God watched over all who believed in Him. Nothing escaped His watchful eye. Tonight He'd known the danger Emma faced, and He hadn't looked away. He'd been here to protect her, and He had done it by using Brock.

The knowledge sent a surge of happiness sweeping through her soul, and in its aftermath it left new hope. Brock had risked his life tonight to save Emma, and that canceled out all the mistakes in the past. Forgiveness had seemed so difficult before, but it didn't seem so now. The hurts of the past were gone, and she had peace like she hadn't known in years. She needed to tell Brock that right away.

She strode toward the gate into the theater, but she stopped about halfway there. Her skin prickled, and chills crept up her spine. Her eyes widened at the frosty sensation drifting through her body. The icy inkling she'd experienced on the beach the day of Jake's murder had returned. That morning someone had been watching her.

Her gaze darted over the enclosed grassy area of the theater, but she was alone. She wiggled her shoulders to shake off the unease attacking her, but it was no use. Her mind told her she was reacting to what had happened here earlier, but her heart told her differently. She didn't know where he was, but she knew he was near. Watching. Waiting. Biding his time until his next opportunity to wreak havoc on her and those she loved.

Slowly, she turned in a circle and scanned the area, trying to find his hiding place. She didn't know where he was, but she knew he was watching. Seeing nothing, she walked back to the gate and stopped.

"I know you're out there," she called out. "I'm not scared of you, but you'd better watch out for me. I'm coming for you, and when I do, you're going to pay for everything you've done on my island."

Straightening to her full height, she exited the theater and walked to the side street where she'd parked her car. Her heart beat in rhythm with her footsteps as she listened for movement behind her. When she reached the car, she unlocked it, climbed inside and cranked the engine.

She'd taunted him and expected him to attack, but he hadn't. Not this time. But he would. She prayed that when he did, she would be ready.

Brock sat at the table on the back porch of the Island Connection Bed-and-Breakfast. No sounds came from inside the

Victorian house. Sam and Tracey Burnett and Dillon McAlister had come back from the festival some time ago, but after inquiring about how he was feeling, they had disappeared inside. Even Treasury had gone to bed.

Tears had run down her cheeks when she thanked him for saving Emma earlier. Her deep commitment to Kate and her sisters had become evident to him since he'd been her guest, and he'd seen how deeply affected she'd been tonight.

He poured himself a glass of lemonade from the pitcher Treasury had brought him and took a sip. The cool liquid soothed his parched throat. He wished something could take away the pain on his arms and chest. He glanced down at the short-sleeved T-shirt he wore and the loose bandages covering his burns. Dr. Hunter had given him some pain medication, but he didn't want to take it until he'd seen Kate. He thought she'd be here by now, and he was beginning to get concerned.

At the flash of Kate's headlights he sat up straight. His heart thudded when she climbed from the car and walked toward the back porch.

The regulation hairdo was gone tonight. In its place her hair tumbled to her shoulders and sparkled in the moonlight. He took a deep breath to calm the excitement he felt at seeing her. Even though he'd understood why she wasn't at the Health Center, he'd wanted her near him all the time he was there. The reality that she was becoming an important part of his life again hit him, and his heart sank. If she knew that, it might undo all the progress he'd made in the last few days toward a friendship with her. He rose and smiled as she stepped onto the back porch.

She looked him over. "How are you feeling?"

"I'm having some pain, but I'll be okay in a few days."

A small oil lamp sat in the middle of the table, and the flickering flame cast a golden glow across her face. Her eyes filled with tears. "Brock, I'll never be able to thank you enough for saving my sister."

He swallowed and shook his head. "You don't have to thank me, Kate. As I told Emma, I'm glad I was there to help."

She stepped closer to him and took his hand. She lifted his arm and studied the bandages. "What did Doc Hunter say?"

Her touch sent electric shocks shooting up his arm, and he grimaced. He longed to wrap her in his arms and forget everything that happened in the past. If only they could go back and undo the events of six years ago.

Reality clicked in his mind. He pulled away and flexed his fingers. "He said the burns were second-degree. I have quite a bit of blistering, but I'll be all right in a few days. The bandages are there to protect the blisters from being broken."

She dropped down in a chair and propped her elbows on the table. Running her fingers into her hair above her temples, she leaned forward. "I've got to find this guy before he hurts someone else."

"Did you have any luck?"

"No. It was as if he disappeared out of the midst of everybody at the festival." She bit on her lip before she glanced up at him. "He sent me a text message right before he threw the firebomb."

Brock walked around to the chair across from her. "What did he say?"

Her eyes filled with tears, and she pulled the phone from her pocket. "It was sent from Doug's cell phone."

Brock dropped down in the chair and exhaled. "Doug's phone?"

"Yes. I nearly panicked when I saw Doug's name. Then I looked up and saw the pirate throw the firebomb." She let out a groan. "Oh, Brock, I've got to catch this guy."

"You will." He leaned forward. He wanted to comfort her,

but he didn't know what to say. His gaze fell on the pitcher that sat on the table. "Do you want a glass of lemonade?"

"No. I just stopped by to see how you're doing and to say thank you. I can't stay long."

"I'm glad you came by." He leaned back in his chair and positioned his arm across his stomach.

Kate stared at the lamp's flame for a moment before she said anything else. "Do you remember what I said to you at the beach the night of Doug's death about trusting God's plan for my life?"

"Yes."

A sob escaped her throat. "Tonight I questioned if I really had put my complete trust in Him to take care of me when I saw Emma on fire. It's one thing to trust God with your own life. It's quite another to trust the lives of those you love to Him."

"I can see how that would be hard. But you say you questioned it. Did you come up with an answer?"

"I got angry, and I told him I couldn't understand why he would put a child in harm's way. It wasn't right for Emma to suffer because somebody hates me." A tear trickled from the corner of her eye. "But He gave me an answer, and I wanted to tell you."

Brock frowned. "Why me?"

"Because you came here to find faith, and you asked me to help you. It's not good if the teacher can't believe the subject she's supposed to be teaching."

Brock leaned forward, and his arm brushed against the side of the table. A rush of pain cascaded through his body. He bit down on his lip before he continued. "What's the answer God gave you?"

She smiled. "His words flashed into my brain as if He was sitting right beside me. He didn't promise we wouldn't have problems, but He did promise He'd be there for us. Tonight He was there in you, Brock. He pushed you onto that stage and saved my sister's life. I wanted you to know that God loves you and kept you from being hurt worse, too."

Her words poured over him and soothed his troubled spirit. He blinked back the moisture in his eyes. "I've never thought of myself as someone God could use."

She leaned forward and stared into his eyes. "But you are, Brock. He's been using you for years in your job, in your new relationship with your father and now He's using you to help me understand how I can't go through my life holding grudges and being unforgiving toward people around me."

His breath caught in his throat. "What are you trying to tell me, Kate?"

"I've been miserable because I haven't been able to forgive you for breaking our engagement. Now I'm beginning to see that maybe you weren't the only one at fault. There might have been some compromises we could have chosen, but we didn't. Over the past week and especially tonight, I saw that you're not the person I've hated for the past six years. I think God brought you here to show me that, and I want you to know I've forgiven you for the hurts in the past." She took a big breath. "And I want to ask you to forgive me for my attitude toward you."

He sat in shocked silence for a moment before he spoke. "Do you mean it, Kate?"

She nodded. "I do."

He reached for her hand, and she laced her fingers with his. "I forgave you a long time ago. I'm thankful that you've been able to forgive me. That's what I wanted when I came here. If your faith in God has helped you do that, then I want that same faith. I'm working on it, Kate."

She smiled and rose to her feet. "Give it time. It will come." She paused. "I had intended to tell you tonight I wanted you to leave. Now that's changed. I'm glad you're here."

He pushed to his feet and moved to stand beside her. His heart felt lighter than it had in years. He stared down into her eyes, smiled, and put his uninjured arm around her shoulder. She didn't resist when he pulled her toward him but stepped closer and laid her head on his chest.

"I don't want to cause your burns to hurt," she murmured.

He pressed his cheek against the side of her head. The fruity fragrance of her shampoo drifted up, causing him to recall other moments when they'd stood like this. "You aren't hurting me. This feels so right."

Brock hadn't felt such happiness in years. The journey toward regaining her friendship had begun when he arrived on the island. Tonight it had advanced to the point of forgiveness on her part. Maybe what he hadn't dared let himself dream could come true. Someday their relationship might progress to something more.

He couldn't think about that now, though. For the time being he was content to hold her in his arms and dream of what the future might bring.

TWELVE

The hot air enveloped Kate and made her gasp as she stepped from the cool interior of the police station into the Saturday heat. Even with the village streets and the festival booths crowded with tourists, it had been a quiet day so far on Ocracoke, and she hoped it would continue during her afternoon patrol.

A seagull squawked overhead, and she peered upward at the bird. Its flight path indicated a destination at the marina. No doubt it was off to join the feathered flock one could see often at the harbor—seagulls waiting for the return of the charter fishing boats that took tourists to sea for the day.

Soon the pilings at the marina would be covered with birds waiting to snatch a bite of the scraps left after the day's catch had been cleaned. Although it had always been one of her favorite times of day, it now saddened her to see the restless birds waiting for a small tidbit.

Very different from the days when she was a child and the birds didn't look like beggars waiting for a handout. Then the boats that left the harbor were headed toward deep water so they could sell their catch to the mainland canneries, and they returned with huge catches.

Her island was different now. The boats at the marina made only quick trips to sea as they competed for the money the tourists brought to the local economy. No doubt about it: life had been perfect on Ocracoke before the tourists discovered it.

Kate climbed in her car and followed the bird's path. Her destination was the same—the harbor. The ferry would dock in a few minutes, and the truck transporting the fireworks for tonight's big show would unload. She wanted to be on the scene when it did.

Her thoughts turned to Brock as she drove toward the marina. Although he'd protested he felt well enough to accompany her today, she had insisted he stay at Treasury's out of the heat, and to rest. A smile curled her lips. She had, however, agreed to accompany him to dinner at the Markata, the priciest restaurant on the island, tonight.

Kate pulled to a stop at the marina at the same time the ferry eased into its dock. A small tractor trailer containing the fireworks, the only vehicle onboard as a safety precaution, sat on deck. Within minutes the crew had the huge boat in place and the truck rumbled from the ferry. It turned left at the main village street and pulled into a parking lot that fronted the shoreline. Kate drove toward the area and stopped beside the truck as two workers climbed from the cab of the big delivery truck.

Kate stepped out of the car and approached the men. "Any problems crossing Pamlico Sound?"

The men shook their heads. The older of the two held out his hand. "I'm Pete Hodges and this is Jeff Wallace. We're the delivery guys. Where is the setup crew?"

She shook hands with Pete and Jeff, then glanced at her watch. "They're supposed to be here at one o'clock. So they should be here any minute."

Pete pulled off the cap he wore and mopped at the perspiration on his brow. "It's a mighty hot day to be setting up a fireworks display. What time is the show tonight?"

"Ten o'clock. It takes our crew about seven hours to set up each year, so they should have enough time to get it done." She smiled. "The crowds don't like to be kept waiting, you know."

Jeff chuckled and glanced at Pete. "We know about that. It happened at the last place we delivered to, and the crowd got mean."

A car pulled into the parking lot, and Russell Johnson and his wife, Rose, got out. Two young men climbed from the back door on the opposite side of the vehicle. They turned toward Kate, and she did a double take. Mike Thornton and Kyle Johnson stared at her over the top of the car.

Russell grinned when he saw Kate, and she walked closer. "Hi, Russell. Rose. Glad to see you." She inclined her head toward Mike and Kyle. "You've got some new crew members this year."

Rose pointed to Kyle. "That's our grandson Kyle, and of course you know Mike Thornton."

She glanced at Mike, who dropped his gaze and turned his back to Kate. "I do. In fact I've met Kyle, too." She pulled her attention away and pointed to the tractor trailer. "Glad to see your crew is ready, Russell. The truck just got here with the delivery. So I guess you guys are ready to go. Do you need anything from me?"

Russell shook his head. "No, we've been doing this so many years, it just comes naturally now." He pointed to Kyle and Mike. "I've got me some trainees this year. Kyle has wanted to help with this for years. His dad finally gave in and let him come down from Raleigh. He met Mike down at the marina, and he wanted to learn, too. But first we got to get this stuff unloaded."

"Do you need me to help?" Kate asked.

"No. We'll take care of it, but I forgot to stop at the Island General Store and get us some water. We'll need it this afternoon." Russell pulled some money from his pocket and turned to the two young men. "Kyle, you and Mike go over there and get us some bottled water and a few snacks. When you get back, you can help us unload."

Kyle grinned and took the money. "Now don't you get started, Granddad, before we get back."

Russell laughed. "Don't worry. You'll have plenty to do."

Mike Thornton followed Kyle back to the car, and they drove from the parking lot. Kate watched them go before she turned back to Russell. "We're shorthanded after Doug's death, and I have some rounds to make. If you're sure I can't help, I'm going to get back on patrol. I'll check back with you in a little while." She turned to leave but stopped. "I don't have to remind you to keep all tourists out of this parking lot."

Russell nodded. "I heard about what happened last night, but you don't have to worry. I've been doing this a lot of years, Kate. Some of the volunteer firefighters are coming to help us, too, so we won't let anyone get close."

"Good. See you later."

Kate hesitated before she got into her squad car and glanced back at Russell. Jeff and Pete swung the big doors of the trailer open, and the three men peered inside. Rose walked over and said something to Russell, and he nodded.

A gust of wind blew off the water, and chill bumps raced up Kate's arm. The strange feeling she'd experienced twice before had returned. She glanced around the parking lot and the street that ran beside it, but she saw no one.

She didn't like the idea of leaving the crew alone, but they wouldn't be alone. Russell said some of the volunteer firefighters were coming to help. Maybe she should stay, too. But she couldn't. Calvin needed to sleep because he had night duty, and that left her to take care of everything else.

With the bank closed on Saturday and tourists' sales in

the shops and booths skyrocketing, several merchants had requested a police escort to use the night deposit box. It made the shop owners feel safer if a deputy was with them when they carried large amounts of money to a deserted bank parking lot and had to get out of their car to open the night deposit. And with the things that had happened on the island in the past few days, none of the locals felt safe.

She glanced at the group again and shook her head. She was being ridiculous. Russell was a retired park ranger who had settled on Ocracoke, and he had backed up the Sheriff's Department on many occasions. He would keep a close watch and make sure that no one got too close to the truck.

Kate drove back through the village and pulled into the parking lot at the Island General Store. She got out, climbed the steps to the store and went inside.

Kyle, holding a basket loaded with bottled water, cookies and chips, stood beside Mike in a long line of customers at the cash register. She smiled and waved at them as she headed to the back of the store to the office of Sam Isaacs, the store owner. She stopped at the open door and looked in at Sam, sitting behind a battered wooden desk.

"Ready to make your deposit, Sam?"

Sam jumped in surprise, and he glanced up at Kate, a startled expression on his face. He took a deep breath before he straightened the glasses on his bulbous nose and pushed to his feet. With a glare directed at her, he pulled the white apron he wore down over his rotund stomach and came around the desk toward her. "You scared the living daylights out of me, Kate. You ought to be ashamed of yourself."

Kate laughed and waved a hand in dismissal. "I'm sorry. Are you ready to go make your deposit?"

Frowning, Sam picked up a bank bag from his desk and followed Kate out of the office. He'd only taken a few steps before he stopped, muttered something under his breath and strode to a table piled high with beach towels. He frowned at the sight of the unfolded towels scattered about the table. "Would you look at that? The dingbatters have rifled through every display today and left them in a mess."

Kate cast a quick glance around and moved closer to the paunchy storekeeper. "Not so loud, Sam. Somebody will hear."

Sam glanced around at the customers in his store, then leaned toward her. "Why should I care? Ever since I can remember that's what we been calling people that don't live on our island."

"Well, you shouldn't be calling your customers—"

Her words were cut short by a loud explosion in the distance. Before she could react, a second *boom* rocked the building, sending items on shelves plummeting to the floor. Customers in the store froze in place.

Sam's eyebrows arched, and his face paled. "What was that?"

Kate's heart dropped to the pit of her stomach. There was no doubt in her mind what they'd just heard. "It sounded like the—"

Before she could finish, a chime from her cell phone signaled an incoming text message. She flipped it open and stared in horror at Doug's name displayed as the sender. The message sent chills rippling through her body.

Have you seen The Dock of the Bay? It's the perfect ending for the festival.

She snapped the phone closed and bolted for the door. Kyle and Mike stared at her with wide eyes and ran behind her to the front porch of the store. Outside she glanced in the direction of the marina and spotted a large mushroom cloud of smoke rising in the sky.

"That's coming from the marina!" Mike Thornton shouted.

"My grandparents," Kyle groaned. The basket filled with snacks dropped from his hand. A bottle of water rolled past Kate's feet as she dashed down the front steps toward the squad car.

Lisa's voice crackled on her lapel mic before she could start the car. "Code 3. Code 3. Parking lot by ferry. EMS on the way."

Kate turned on the siren and careened from the store's parking lot. Everywhere she looked people ran in the direction of the marina. A car pulled out from a side street. Kate blew the horn and swerved around it. She had to get to the marina before the crowd converged on the area.

But what would she find? What about Russell and Rose? And Pete and Jeff? A few minutes ago she'd been talking with them. Would they be there when she arrived?

It only took a few minutes to navigate the traffic on the clogged main street before she caught sight of the parking lot at the end of the marina. Black smoke still boiled up. The fire truck with the volunteer firefighters Russell had mentioned pulled into the lot in front of her.

She cut her siren, skidded to a stop and jumped from the squad car. The wail of an ambulance sliced through the afternoon air. It sped into the parking lot and came to a stop next to the fire truck.

Long strips of metal that had once been the sides of the trailer lay scattered in a circle around the vehicle's charred base. The debris, fanned around what had once been a tractor trailer, looked as if some giant titans had released pickup sticks in preparation for an afternoon game. Fire blazed all along the shoreline, and patches of red flickered in the debris.

Kate spotted Russell and Rose lying in the midst of the

wreckage. She started toward them, but a firefighter grabbed her arm. "No, Kate. Let us make sure there's no danger from further explosions before you get closer."

She stopped and looked over her shoulder. He was right. They had their job to do, and the paramedics would take care of the victims. Her job was to keep the crowds back, but she didn't know how one lone deputy could do it.

Then she saw them. The crew from the ferry ran toward her, and several hotel and shop owners rushed from the other direction. The island residents were responding as they always did when help was needed. She had no doubt other volunteers would arrive shortly. Their job at present was to keep the crowds that hurried toward the parking lot from getting close to the scene while the firefighters and paramedics did their jobs.

All she could do was hope that they weren't too late to save the lives of the four people she'd talked to no more that fifteen minutes ago.

Brock had just sat down with a glass of iced tea and the day's newspaper at the table on the back porch of Treasury's house when he heard the explosion. Startled, he jumped to his feet. The second explosion sent him hurrying down the steps and around the house to the front yard. He stared in the direction he thought the sound had come from and spied a black cloud of smoke drifting upward.

Treasury, holding a broom in her hands, ran onto the front porch. "What was that?"

"I don't know, but I have a feeling it's something bad."

Treasury gazed at the cloud. "That looks like the marina area. Didn't Kate say something about the fireworks being delivered today? Do you think some of them might have been set off?"

He gasped and almost bent double at the pain that kicked

him in the stomach. Kate! She said she had to be there when the truck rolled off the ferry. What if she had been involved in that explosion?

Panic surged through his body, paralyzing him with fear. His chest tightened, and he struggled to breathe. He had to find out if Kate was all right. He took a step toward his car but stopped. If a disaster had occurred, the streets might be blocked with emergency vehicles and the cars of sightseers. The fastest way to get there was to run.

"I'll go find out what it was," he called out to Treasury, as he dashed into the street.

It was less than a mile from Treasury's house to the marina. No problem for a man used to jogging several miles every day. But today the distance seemed longer than the marathon he'd run last summer. His heart beat in rhythm with the pounding of his feet on the street's surface, and he willed his body to move faster.

When he came closer to the marina he realized he'd been right. Cars lined the sides of the street, and he could see people gathered along the edge of the parking lot by the ferry. He slowed his steps and moved cautiously through the gathered onlookers. His chest heaved, more from fright than the run, and he eased forward. If Kate was among the injured, how could he face it? Being with her again had been the best thing that had happened to him in years.

Her words about her faith that God would take care of her even in death drifted through his mind. He stopped at the edge of the crowd and put his hands over his eyes. Her faith helped her face each day and what it brought without fear. He wanted that, too.

A breeze from the ocean ruffled his hair. It reminded him of her words that God was like the wind; you couldn't see Him but you could feel Him. His heartbeat drummed in his ears, and he opened his eyes and stared upward.

God, he prayed, *if You're there, give me the strength to face whatever is on the other side of these people.*

His heartbeat slowed, and his body relaxed. It was as if the wind itself had seeped through his pores and blown away the panic he'd felt a few minutes earlier. Now a peace like he'd never known filled him. He opened his eyes and made his way through the crowd to the edge of the parking lot.

The area before him looked like something one might see in the aftermath of an action movie explosion. Emergency vehicles with flashing lights dotted the parking lot. Men and women, some of whom he recognized from island shops, faced the crowd and blocked a better view of the scene. But where was Kate?

Then he saw her about halfway across the parking lot talking to two men. She glanced over her shoulder at the EMS workers behind her and shouted to them, "Here are two doctors who are vacationing on the island. They want to help."

His knees sagged with relief, and he started toward her. He was almost there when a paunchy man wearing a long, white apron blocked his way. "Sorry, mister, you'll have to wait with the rest of the crowd."

At the edge of the parking lot a man inched onto the pavement and trained his camera on the scene. Kate frowned and yelled at a volunteer who stood nearby. "Try to keep anyone from photographing the scene. We still have victims here." Kate looked in Brock's direction and waved. "It's okay, Sam," she called out. "Let him through."

One of the firefighters ran up to her, and she turned her attention to him. She listened as he spoke, then pulled out her cell phone. She said a few words, then nodded and closed the phone.

The paramedic headed back toward his truck. "Thanks, Kate."

Brock took a step forward but stopped at the sound of a shout behind him. "Kyle, no! Don't go down there!"

Brock turned to see a young man running across the parking lot with another one chasing him. He recognized Kyle Johnson and Mike Thornton, the boys he'd met when the missing boat from the marina was recovered.

Kate caught sight of the two and ran toward them. She and Mike both grabbed Kyle who was now crying hysterically. "Granddad! Grandmother!"

Kate put her arm around the boy and spoke quietly to him. He shook his head, struggled to get loose from her grip and screamed louder. Mike's father, Ean, ran from the crowd toward his son. When he stopped, Kate spoke to him for a moment. Ean nodded, and then he and Mike pulled the grief-stricken boy from the scene.

Brock's legs trembled as he walked toward her. She'd never looked more beautiful to him, but he recognized something else in her appearance. Not only was she an attractive woman, she was also a police officer who looked every inch the professional.

Ever since he'd been here he'd seen how highly she was regarded among the island residents. With a confidence he'd seen in few seasoned officers, she stood in the midst of chaos dispensing orders and responding to the needs of the emergency workers and family members with an authority that left little doubt who was in charge.

The truth hit him. She belonged here. Not in a big city on a police force, but on the small island with the people she'd known and loved all her life. She'd wanted him to share that with her, and he'd refused. He'd paid the price for that decision. Seeing her now made him wish he could roll back time and undo that mistake, but he couldn't.

She gazed sharply at him when he stopped in front of her. "Brock, what are you doing here? You should be resting."

He shook his head. "I want to help. Tell me what to do."

"You can help us keep the crowds back. The ambulance will be heading to the Health Center in a few minutes. We have a helicopter coming in to take the survivor to a hospital."

Brock glanced over the carnage. "How many people died?"

Her eyes filled with tears before she blinked them away and straightened her shoulders. "Three. Russell and Rose Johnson and one of the delivery drivers, Pete Hodges. The other delivery man is critical, but he's alive."

"What happened?"

"I don't know for sure. One of the workers on the ferry said he saw the men in the parking lot open the door of the trailer. He said they stepped around to the side for a moment, and out of nowhere this jogger appeared. He didn't see where the jogger came from—he was just suddenly running across the parking lot. He ran up behind the trailer and threw something in, and then took off."

"Did the ferry worker see what the jogger threw inside?"

"No, but Russell yelled at him. The guy didn't look back. He ran out of the parking lot and onto the street. Russell walked to the back of the truck, and then the whole thing exploded. The second blast sent the big cloud of smoke upward."

The memory of the firebomb hitting the stage the night before flashed in Brock's mind. "It must have been some kind of incendiary device. Did the ferry worker get a good look at the jogger?"

"No. He wore a jogging suit with a hooded shirt. His head was covered, but he could see sunglasses on the man's face. He couldn't give me a description."

Brock mulled over what Kate had told him. "So our pirate has struck again."

"He sent me another text message from Doug's cell phone. Do you want to see it?"

Brock's heart thudded as she held the phone out to him. He read the message and sighed. "This guy is a piece of work. I've never understood why anyone would want to hurt an innocent person."

"Me, either. This time he's gone too far, though. I've talked with Sheriff Baxter. Agents from the Bureau of Alcohol, Tobacco, Firearms and Explosives are on their way. This investigation is going to be in their hands. Calvin and I will assist them."

Relief flowed through Brock. "Good. Maybe this guy will concentrate on avoiding federal agents and leave you alone."

Kate sighed. "Maybe so. We'll have to see." She glanced around. "It looks like the ambulance is getting ready to leave. Let's clear a path for him."

Brock moved to assist Kate. He couldn't help but be relieved. Whoever was causing all this mayhem on Ocracoke had gotten out of control. Maybe by working together the two agencies could stop him.

He hoped so. Kate had been placed in too much danger already, and he wanted her safe. Once she was, he had two choices. He could either tell her of his feelings for her, or he could leave. At this point he didn't know which would be better. That was a decision he didn't look forward to making.

THIRTEEN

Kate rubbed her hands over her eyes. She didn't remember when she'd ever been so tired. She glanced at the clock on the wall in the interrogation room at the police station. After midnight, and they were no closer to an answer to the tragedy today than they had been hours ago.

The cold remains of the gallons of coffee they'd consumed sat scattered about the table where for the past five hours she, Calvin and Brock had related the horror of the day to the ATF agents who had arrived in late afternoon. She stifled a yawn and sat up straighter. "Anybody want more coffee?"

Austin Whitman, the ATF agent in charge, looked up from writing on the pad in front of him and shook his head. "None for me." He pinched the bridge of his nose and pushed his glasses up. The lenses magnified his tired eyes. He leaned forward, his arms resting on the table. "Deputy Michaels, when a crime like the one you had today occurs, our agency is authorized to take over the case. That doesn't mean, however, you and your officers will be left out of the loop. Our objective is to help you find the person who's committed the act. Maybe by pooling our resources we can find this crazy killer and put a stop to his wild rampage."

Kate had liked Austin Whitman the minute they had shaken hands. His no-nonsense attitude had come across quickly. She glanced around the table at Austin and the other three agents and nodded. "We're glad you're here. The actions of our perpetrator have gone beyond anything we've experienced before on Ocracoke. We appreciate your help, and we'll work with you any way we can."

Agent Whitman smiled. "Good." He pointed to the map of the island that Kate had laid in the center of the table. "You've marked the spots that our guy has hit. He seems to be all over the place. Since no one has seen his face, it's going to be hard to find him. He could walk right past us on the street, and we wouldn't know. Some of us will be in the crowd at the festival tomorrow..." He glanced at his watch. "Or should I say today, in case he strikes again."

Kate glanced at Brock and Calvin. "We'll be there, too." She pushed back from the table and stood. "If there's nothing else, I think we need to get some sleep and meet back in the morning. Calvin will let us know if we're needed tonight."

The agents stood, and Agent Whitman held out his hand. "We'll see you in the morning." After shaking hands with Kate, he turned to Brock. "It's good to meet you, Detective Gentry. You may be out of your jurisdiction here on Ocracoke, but it's good to have a fellow officer volunteering to help us."

Brock gripped the man's hand. "Thanks. I want to do anything I can."

Kate stared at the two men, who'd seemed to hit it off when the agents first arrived. Brock had always said he wanted to start in a big-city department and then progress to a federal agency. She wondered if that was still in the back of his mind. He hadn't mentioned it since he'd been on the island, but she couldn't imagine he'd given up that goal.

When the agents left the room, Kate turned back to Calvin. "Don't hesitate to call me if you see anything suspicious tonight."

"I won't, but there's something I need to ask you."

"What?"

Calvin touched his lower jaw and winced. "I think I'm developing an abscess in one of my back teeth. I've been in pain for several days, but I didn't say anything because I knew how shorthanded we were. With these agents on the island, would it be okay for me to take off Monday and go to my dentist on the mainland? I don't think I can stand this much longer."

Kate frowned. "You should have told me, Calvin. We would have made arrangements to cover for you."

"I didn't think I should leave, but with federal agents here I thought it might be okay."

Brock pushed up from his chair and yawned. "You'd better get that taken care of. If the infection spreads, you could really be sick."

The memory of her talk with Lisa about Calvin flashed into her mind. Did he really have a bad tooth, or did Calvin only want to meet the woman Lisa had heard him talking with on the phone? The question was on the tip of her tongue, but she couldn't speak it. Calvin had always been an exemplary officer, and she wasn't going to doubt his motives for asking to go to the mainland.

She swallowed back the words she'd almost said. "I agree. So let me know what you find out. I'll be back in the morning to relieve you, and I can cover Monday night if you're still gone."

Calvin opened his mouth to speak but grabbed his jaw and winced again. "Well, if you're sure you can spare me, I think I'll grab a few hours' sleep in the morning after I get off patrol and then take one of the afternoon ferries to the mainland. That way I can be at my dentist's office early Monday morning. He's a good friend, and he always works me in when I show up."

"Let us know how things go and when you'll be back."

"I will. Now I'd better get back on patrol. No telling what's going on over at the Blue Pelican with this being the last night of the festival."

Kate waited for Calvin to leave before she glanced at Brock. "I'll drop you at Treasury's before I head for home."

"Thanks."

As they stepped from the office, the cool night air enveloped them. Kate stopped beside her car, closed her eyes and inhaled. "What a day. I still can't believe that Russell and Rose are dead. I felt so sorry for their grandson."

Brock stood on the opposite side of the car, his hand on the door handle. He stared at her across the roof of the vehicle. "I did, too. But are you really all right? Having this killer send you two text messages from Doug's cell phone must have been rough on you."

"Yeah, it was, but it's made me more determined than ever to catch him. There has to be justice for those who've died. But I suppose there was one good thing to come out of the day."

"What's that?" Brock asked.

She stared at him. "You mentioned Ean Thornton as a possible suspect after his outburst the night we found the stolen boat. After today I know he couldn't be. He knew his son, Mike, was supposed to be helping Russell set up the fireworks display. There's no way he would have done anything that would put his son in danger."

"I guess you're right." Brock bit down on his lip, and his gaze raked her face. In his eyes Kate could see a flicker of something. Sadness? Regret? "I have to tell you something else I was wrong about, Kate."

She tilted her head, her heart pounding at the wounded look on his face. "What?"

"I watched you today at that horrible scene, and I knew you belonged there. I was wrong when I asked you to leave this island. You're a part of it as much as the sand and salt marshes that hold this little piece of earth together. You belong here, and I'm sorry for the hurt I put you through by trying to make you leave."

The words she'd never expected to hear him say shocked Kate into silence. When she didn't answer, Brock jerked the car door open and climbed inside. She wanted to tell him that she'd watched him over the past few days, and she, too, had discovered something. Brock belonged here, too.

She'd seen the way he'd bonded with the island residents, her sisters in particular. It was almost as if the sand had penetrated his body and transformed him into an O'Cocker, the term locals used for those who lived on their small stretch of land.

She knew it, but she could never tell Brock what she saw in him. He had to discover it for himself. That was what she'd wanted six years ago, and now she wanted it again. But she doubted if he would recognize it now any more than he had then.

On Sunday afternoon Kate and Brock sat in the squad car at the edge of the parking lot that was still marked as a crime scene. The ATF agents had been busy all day at the site of yesterday's explosion, but so far they had uncovered nothing new.

Kate glanced at Brock, who had been quiet since she picked him up earlier in the morning. His gloom-and-doom mood had prevailed most of the day, and she couldn't figure it out. The horn of the ferry shook her from her thoughts and turned her attention to the harbor and the arriving ferry. The sun glinted on the white sides of the sleek vessel as it glided into port and slid into its berth.

A long line of cars waited to board as they did every Sunday afternoon. This was the day of the week when most vacationers departed, only to be replaced by those crowded on the incoming ferries to begin their stay on the island. Sometimes it seemed a never-ending cycle, but she knew it would soon change. When fall came, many of the island businesses would close, and the tourist trade would trickle to a small number.

"There's Calvin." Brock's voice interrupted her thoughts. "He doesn't have to worry about making this ferry."

She looked past Brock's pointing finger to the cars waiting to board the ferry and spotted Calvin. He was at the head of the line. "Since we're so remote, islanders who need to get to the mainland are loaded first. I guess it's one of the perks of living here."

Brock glanced around and sighed. "I'd say there are a lot of reasons to like living here."

Kate's eyebrows arched. Was he trying to tell her what she hoped? That he had decided this is where he belonged, too? She wanted to press the question with him, but the fear that she was mistaken kept her silent.

For the next few minutes they watched the cars disembark from the ferry and drive onto the main street that ran through the village. When the last one had left the ship, a worker standing at the boarding ramp motioned for the vehicles to pull forward. Calvin eased his car onto the ramp and drove onto the ferry.

One after another the cars and trucks followed until the last one had boarded. As the ship prepared to push out into Pamlico Sound for its return trip to Swan Quarter on the mainland, Kate caught sight of Calvin climbing the stairs on the outside of the deck to the clubhouse. She thought of all the times she'd sat at a table in that huge room and ridden back and forth on the ferry. To some the trip might seem like an inconvenience, but to her it was part of her life here.

Kate took a deep breath and turned the car's ignition. "I

guess it's time to get back on patrol. I think we'd better check the beach and see if there have been any problems today."

Brock nodded. "Sounds good." He glanced out the window as she drove through the village. "Do you remember how we used to go to the beach on Sunday afternoons? Your mother would always pack us a picnic."

Her heart thumped at the mention of her mother. "I remember."

Brock was silent for a moment. "Emma looks so much like your mother."

"I think so, too, and she's like her in ways other than her appearance. Mother loved animals and was always helping any stray she found. I think of her every time I see Emma with her cat, Rascal. Mother would have made sure he had a home, too."

Brock laughed for the first time all day. "That cat ran under my feet day before yesterday when I was coming out of the bed-and-breakfast and nearly scared me to death."

Kate chuckled and glanced at him. "He's good at that. He does it to me all the time. Treasury says—"

Before she could finish, her phone rang, and she pulled it from the clip on her belt. Betsy's cell phone number flashed on the caller ID. "Hi, Betsy. Do you need something?"

A soft cry of alarm caused Kate to sit up straight. "K-Kate, I'm so sc-scared."

Kate pulled the car to the side of the street and stopped. "What's wrong, Betsy?"

"I can't find Emma."

"Where are you?"

"I'm at home. Emma and I ate lunch with Treasury after church, and then we came home. I told Emma that I needed to get a painting to take back to the booth at the festival and for her to wait for me in the car. When I came back outside, she was gone." Betsy's last words dissolved into tears.

Fear knotted Kate's stomach. "How long has she been gone?"

"About thirty minutes. I looked all through the house, in the yard, then I went out to the beach. She's nowhere to be found. Oh, Kate, what if that man who tried to burn her took her?"

Glancing in the rearview mirror, Kate made a U-turn and headed back through town, the siren on her squad car blaring. "We don't know that's happened, Betsy. Brock and I will be there in a few minutes. If we don't find her, I'll call the rescue team to help us search."

"Oh, Kate," Betsy cried. "Please hurry. I'm so scared."

Kate accelerated the car and looked over at Brock, who clutched the car seat. His wide eyes told her he understood what had happened. He licked his lips. "Has Emma disappeared?"

Kate bit her lip, nodded and blinked back tears. This was no time to get emotional. Betsy sounded almost hysterical, and Kate needed to stay focused so they could find Emma. The thought of her being the victim of the madman who was terrorizing the island made her nauseous. She'd seen Russell's and Rose's bodies as well as Doug's. She couldn't let that happen to her little sister.

The car roared down the road to the house Kate shared with her sisters, and she skidded to a stop at the end of the driveway. Betsy stood in the yard. Tears streaked her face, and she clutched her hands in front of her.

When Kate stepped from the car, Betsy rushed to her. "Kate, we've got to find her. I'll never forgive myself for leaving her alone if something's happened to her."

Brock touched Betsy's shoulder. "We'll find her, Betsy. I don't know where she is, but I have a gut feeling that she's okay."

Tears filled Betsy's eyes. "I hope you're right."

Kate scanned the area for anything that would give her a clue as to what had happened to Emma. She spotted Emma's footprints in the sandy soil and pointed to them. "It looks like she might have gone toward the beach."

Betsy's face paled. "What if she went in the water and the riptide took her out to sea?"

Kate frowned at her sister. "We can't think like that." She strode toward the break in the ridge that led onto the beach. "Come on, Brock. Let's see what we can find."

They climbed the ridge and stepped onto the beach. All that Kate could see in either direction was a long stretch of sand and the water rolling in. She turned back to Brock. "Maybe we should go in different directions. You search the beach area to our left, and I'll go to our right."

He nodded. "That sounds good. If you find anything, call me on my cell phone, and I'll do the same."

"I think we should keep in touch. Let me…" Kate frowned. "What was that I heard?"

Brock shook his head. "I didn't hear anything but the waves crashing on the shore."

"No, listen." They stood silent for a moment before Kate's eyebrows arched, and she turned to him. "I heard it again. It sounds like someone calling my name."

They turned and stared up the beach. Kate squinted and shielded her eyes from the sun. In the distance she could make out a figure running toward them. As it got closer, the image dissolved into the form of a child, and then into Emma.

Emma ran toward them, Rascal in her arms. "Kate! Kate!" she shouted. The ocean obscured the rest of what she was saying.

Kate and Brock sprinted toward her. Both reached her at the same time, but Kate grabbed Emma and hugged her. Between them, Rascal squirmed to jump out of Emma's arms, but she held on to him.

"K-Kate, I—I—I f-found it." Emma panted for breath, making it difficult to understand what she was saying.

Frowning, Kate knelt in front of Emma, took the child by the shoulders and held her at arms' length. Now that Emma was safe, her fear had changed to anger. "What do you mean running off and not telling Betsy? You scared us to death."

"It was Rascal's fault. He ran away from me and wouldn't come back. I called and called him, but he just ran down the beach. I had to go get him."

Kate gave Emma a little shake. "No, you didn't. Don't ever go off without telling us. Do you understand?"

Tears trickled down Emma's cheeks. "I didn't mean to make you mad. I thought you'd be happy because I found it."

"Found what?"

"Blackbeard's treasure."

Kate gasped and glanced up at Brock, who looked as perplexed as she felt. She frowned and looked back at Emma. "What are you talking about?"

Emma wiped a grubby hand across her eyes and tightened her grip on Rascal, who still tried to escape her grasp. "Rascal ran and ran. I chased him all the way to Calvin's house, and I saw him crawl through a loose board at the bottom of Calvin's boathouse and go inside."

Kate scowled at Emma. "You didn't go in Calvin's boathouse, did you? You know how careful he is with his boat."

Emma scrunched her eyes shut, and the tears shot out. "But I had to, Kate. I had to get Rascal. I ran around the deck of the boathouse and tried all the windows until I found one that I could slide open, and I climbed in. Rascal ran under some old blankets that were piled in the corner of the walkway around the boat slip. When I pulled them back, a box next to Rascal tipped over, and part of Blackbeard's treasure fell out."

Kate glanced up at Brock, and he dropped to his knees beside Emma. He put his hand on her shoulder and leaned closer. "We don't understand, Emma. You say you found Blackbeard's treasure. How did you know what it was?"

"Because I've heard Grady tell about the treasure for as long as I can remember." Emma tilted her head to one side. "But it doesn't really look like what Grady said. And it wasn't like the pirate's chest that we had in the play. It was just an old box. Rascal sat down next to it and purred, and I emptied it all out on the floor and looked through it. There was all kinds of stuff in it just like Grady told me. You know, things that a pirate would steal. There were rings, and earrings, and bracelets."

"Did you put everything back like you found it?" Kate asked.

"Yes."

Kate put her finger under Emma's chin and tilted her face up. "Emma, I've told you and told you there isn't a treasure. That's just a story Grady tells the tourists. You probably found an old box of jewelry that belonged to Calvin's mother. She died a year ago, and Calvin brought all her belongings here from her home in Virginia." She stood and dusted the sand from the knees of her uniform. "Come on, Emma. We need to let Betsy know we found you."

Emma hung her head and dug her toe in the sand. Her lips protruded in a pout. "It was a treasure. I know it was." She jerked her head up, and her eyes grew wide. "Oh, no. I forgot."

Kate had taken a step to leave, but she stopped and faced Emma. "What?"

"I tried one of the bracelets on Rascal for a collar. I forgot to put it back."

Kate sighed and moved back to where Emma stood. "How

could you do that? Now we're really going to have to apologize to Calvin. Let me see it."

Emma held the cat up, and Kate and Brock leaned forward to get a good look.

Brock gave a low whistle. "Wow, would you look at that. Calvin's mother must have had some nice jewelry."

Disbelief kicked Kate in the stomach, and her mouth gaped open. After a moment, she swallowed and glanced at Brock. "I don't think we're going to have to apologize to Calvin at all."

Brock frowned. "What do you mean?"

Kate raised a trembling finger and pointed to the bracelet that circled Rascal's neck. The emeralds and diamonds sparkled in the afternoon sun exactly like she'd imagined they would when she first saw the picture Sheriff Baxter had sent of items stolen in the mainland burglaries.

"Calvin needs to explain how a twenty-five-thousand-dollar bracelet that was reported stolen in a home robbery on the mainland found its way into his boathouse."

Brock stared at her as if she'd lost her mind. His gaze flitted from her to the bracelet and back to her face. "You've got to be kidding."

Kate patted Rascal's head, slid her fingers down to the catch of the bracelet and unfastened it. The gems winked at her as she held the bracelet up for Brock to see. "Emma, was there a lot of jewelry in Blackbeard's treasure?"

Emma nodded. "There was a big box full."

Kate shook her head in silent protest. It couldn't be true. Calvin was a trusted law enforcement officer. Thoughts of all the times she, Calvin and Doug had spent together drifted through her mind. They called themselves the Ocracoke Trio. Had Calvin been laughing at her and Doug all that time?

They had trusted Calvin completely and depended on him in dangerous situations. The thought that he might be a thief seemed too ridiculous to even entertain. Yet she held the evidence in her hand. Why would he have a stolen bracelet and, according to Emma, quite a bit more jewelry in a box in his boathouse?

Something else niggled at the back of her mind. It was a piece of information that could be important, but what was it? She wracked her brain, and it popped into her mind. She smiled at the memory of her conversation with Lisa after Doug's death. The Lakeview Lodge on the mainland. Who had Calvin really been meeting there?

Brock touched her shoulder, and she turned to stare at him. "What are you going to do?"

She took a deep breath and straightened her shoulders. "I need to get in touch with Sheriff Baxter right away and tell him to detain Calvin for questioning when the ferry docks at Swan Quarter, and also to have a deputy check out who Calvin has been meeting at the Lakeview Lodge in Swan Quarter."

"I've never heard you mention the Lakeview Lodge. How does that tie in?"

"The burglaries haven't been the work of one person. Maybe someone at that motel can tell us who Calvin has been meeting there." She glanced at her watch. "The ferry left about thirty minutes ago. So we still have two hours before it gets to shore. If Sheriff Baxter can get me a search warrant for Calvin's house and boathouse right away, we may find more evidence before he ever gets off that boat."

Kate took Emma by the hand and hurried back down the beach toward their house. Her father had always told her there was nothing lower than a law officer who violated the trust the people put in him by breaking the law. She hadn't believed that could happen to a deputy on her island, but now it probably had. The thought made her sick.

She lengthened her stride, and Emma ran to keep up with

FOURTEEN

Five hours later Brock stood beside Austin Whitman in the back room of the police station and stared at the items spread across a long table in the center. An array of watches, bracelets, rings and earrings covered half the table, while the other end held an assortment of digital cameras, video recorders and photographic equipment. A table set against the wall held power tools, media players and several laptops.

Brock took a sip of the coffee from the cup he held and chuckled. "Calvin has been a busy boy."

The agent nodded. "Yeah, but according to Kate there are a lot of other items reported stolen that weren't found. He must have a fence somewhere that takes this stuff off his hands."

"Maybe Sheriff Baxter can get him to tell how he's been getting rid of the stuff. Kate said they picked Calvin up when he drove off the ferry. They're questioning him right now."

Brock caught a glimpse of Kate as she walked by the open door to the room. She held her cell phone to her ear and appeared to be in deep conversation.

He wished they could get a few minutes alone to talk. So much had happened since they returned from the beach that he'd barely had a moment with her. Since his name wasn't listed on the search warrant, he hadn't been allowed to accompany Kate and the agents on the search of Calvin's property.

Although he'd been disappointed, he knew she was right. After all, he had no official capacity on the island, and the ATF agents did.

Kate reappeared at the door and placed her cell phone back in the clip on her belt. A big smile curled her lips. "I've been on the phone with Sheriff Baxter. Calvin's in shock that he's been arrested, and he's scared."

Brock chuckled and glanced at Austin. "Good. Maybe he'll talk."

Kate's eyes sparkled, and she glanced from one to the other. "He already has, and what he's said has tied up a lot of loose ends for us."

Brock and Austin walked around the table and stopped in front of her. "Like what?" Brock asked.

"Let's go sit in my office, and I'll catch you up on everything." Kate turned and walked out the door with Brock and Austin right behind.

In her office, Kate plopped down in the chair behind her desk and motioned for them to have seats. When they were settled, she leaned forward and folded her arms on the table. "Well, for starters, Sheriff Baxter had a deputy question the manager at the Lakeview Lodge before the ferry landed. The man gave descriptions of two men whom Calvin had been meeting there. One of them sounded much like Jake Morgan. The other one he described as a young man with long hair, in his early twenties, with a faint scar running across his cheek from his earlobe toward his nose."

Brock sat up straighter. "Mike Thornton?"

Kate arched her eyebrows. "Sounds like him, doesn't it?"

Agent Whitman frowned. "Mike Thornton? Wasn't he supposed to help set up the fireworks display?"

Kate nodded. "He was."

"Does Sheriff Baxter think Mike and Jake were involved with Calvin in the burglary ring?" Brock asked.

"Yes, but it gets better." Kate's eyes sparkled as she glanced from one to the other. "They've been questioning Calvin for the past two hours at the station in Swan Quarter. When they told him they knew about the meetings at the Lakeview Lodge, Calvin got really nervous and said he wanted a lawyer."

Disappointment surged through Brock. "So he quit talking?"

Kate grinned and shook her head. "No, Calvin knows the law. He spoke with his lawyer for a while before they called Sheriff Baxter back in. The lawyer told them that Calvin would plead guilty to the burglary charges, and he could give them the name of Jake's killer. But only if he wasn't charged in the murder."

Brock relaxed and glanced at Austin. "So he wanted to make a deal. Did they agree?"

Kate nodded. "The district attorney okayed it, and Calvin told the whole story. It seems that one night Calvin interrupted Jake selling drugs to Mike. When he started to arrest them, Jake told Calvin he could help him make a lot of money. He'd been doing small robberies for years, but he was ready to go bigger. The more he talked, the more interested Calvin was, and he decided he'd like some quick money, too."

Austin leaned forward in his chair. "How does Mike Thornton figure into this?"

"He'd developed a bad cocaine problem while he was at school, and he was into Jake for a lot of money. Jake told him he could work his debt off by helping him with the robberies. So, the three of them began planning where they'd strike. With three of them working together, they could rob homes at the same time all across the county."

Brock smiled at Kate. "Does Sheriff Baxter want you to arrest Mike for burglary?"

She shook her head. "No. He wants me to arrest him for murder and for assault on an officer."

Brock bolted upright in the chair and stared at Kate. "Murder?"

"Yes. Calvin is willing to testify that he was present on the beach with Jake and Mike the night Jake was murdered. They were arguing because Jake had cut off Mike's cocaine supply. Calvin turned and started back to his car when he heard a shot. He ran back and found Mike standing over Jake's body. He'd shot him in the back. Calvin told Mike he didn't want anything to do with murder, and he left. Later when he found out that I had been shot at on the beach, Calvin went to Mike, and Mike said he never intended to kill me. He just wanted to throw a scare into me."

The longer Kate talked, the more concerned Brock became. "Wanted to scare you? Why?"

"Because he thinks I've picked on him ever since he was a teenager. He wanted to get back at me. And we know he had the opportunity to be at the beach that morning. Remember? He was late to work when the boat from the marina was stolen."

"That's right! And he acted so cocky out at the ferry station when you tried to question him." Brock gave a snort of disgust. "I wonder what he'll think when you arrest him."

Kate bit her bottom lip, and her forehead wrinkled in thought. "I couldn't figure out how the shooter at the beach disappeared so quickly. Now it all makes sense. Mike's driven all over this island for years and knows every back road and path. He must have cut off on one from the main road without Doug seeing him and then driven back to town and showed up late to work at the marina."

Austin nodded. "So Calvin decided he'd better play ball with the police and get a lighter sentence."

"Like I said, Calvin is smart. He knows that the sentence for murder in North Carolina is life in prison with no parole, while home burglary with no one in the house is a Class G felony. The punishment for that is only four and a half years." She grinned. "But then he's going to have multiple charges."

Brock shook his head. "Are you saying that it's possible that Calvin can be out of prison in less than five years?"

Kate pushed to her feet. "That's the law, and Calvin knew it. He denies that he and Mike are involved in the other murders on the island, though, and I believe him." Kate adjusted her duty belt and sighed. "Now I've got to go arrest Mike Thornton. It's not going to be easy. His father is going to try and stop me. Sheriff Baxter is faxing a copy of the search warrant for the Thornton house. I'm sure the judge who is signing these for us will be glad when we're through."

"Did you list the other two agents and me on the search warrant?" Austin asked Kate.

"I did."

"Good. Then let's go." He glanced at Brock. "Detective Gentry, why don't you join us on this one? You can't go inside, but you can watch from the sidelines."

Brock smiled and pushed to his feet. "I wouldn't miss it for the world."

He followed Kate from her office. As they passed Lisa's desk, he noticed that Lisa wasn't there. He knew she had come in earlier and had heard her talking with Kate. He pointed to the dispatch area. "Where's Lisa? I saw her earlier."

"She went home. She's very upset over Calvin's arrest," Kate responded. He waited for her to explain, but she didn't say anything else.

When they were seated in Kate's squad car, Brock swiveled

in the seat and stared at her. "Kate, I'm glad you've uncovered the burglary ring and the answers to Jake's murder. But have you thought about the fact that we still don't know who's been targeting you?"

She sighed and turned the ignition. "I have. Mike couldn't have been watching from the fishing skiff that morning at the beach and shooting at me at the same time. And I saw him at the store when the fireworks truck exploded. I've tried to think who else it might be. Sam Burnett has a hooded sweatshirt, and Clay Phillips was nearby when the killer left a note in my car. Those suspicions aren't enough to prove anything, though."

Brock stared at her profile. The muscle in her jaw twitched, and he reached over and squeezed her arm. "Don't worry. We'll figure it out."

She glanced down at his hand on her arm, and then her gaze drifted up to stare into his eyes. "We will, but all we can do is take care of one thing at a time. Right now I have to arrest Mike Thornton. After that, we can concentrate on finding out who has committed four murders on Ocracoke."

He settled back in the seat and fastened his seat belt as the car pulled into the street. His heart raced at the word she'd used. *We.* It sounded as if she wanted him to help her, and the thought sent ripples of happiness through him. Together they would find this crazy killer.

Sheriff Baxter's office had been shorthanded before all the problems on the island. Now Kate was the only deputy left. The ATF agents would be here for a few days yet as they investigated the fireworks explosion, but it might take longer than that to discover who wanted to kill Kate.

Brock glanced out the window as the car sped toward the Thornton house, and a thought that had been drifting through his mind took root. He still had several weeks of vacation left, but it didn't matter how long it took to find this guy. He wasn't leaving this island until he was sure that Kate was safe. Then he'd leave, but only if she wanted him to.

Out of the corner of his eye, Brock studied Kate all the way to the Thornton house. He wondered what she was thinking. There wasn't a flicker of emotion on her face.

That was one of the things about her he'd always admired and yet at times despised. In an emergency she could respond without her personal feelings interfering. However, when they had faced their breakup six years ago, she had buried her emotions so deeply at times that he couldn't reach her. Now she was on her way to arrest a young man she'd known ever since he was born. He wondered how she really felt about that.

She stopped the car in front of a large Victorian home and took a deep breath. "This is the Thornton home," she said. "When I was a child, I thought this was the most beautiful house on the island. I love the gingerbread trim that gives it so much character."

Brock didn't know what to say. He glanced over his shoulder at the sound of another car coming to a stop. "Austin and the agents just got here."

She started to get out of the car but frowned and turned back to him. "Brock, I appreciate all you've done to help me, but..."

He held up a hand and smiled. "Don't worry. I'll stay out of your way. I'm not about to jeopardize any evidence you find. I don't want a defense attorney getting it thrown out because an unauthorized person joined the search."

She smiled. "Thank you."

They stepped from the car, and Kate led the way up the flagstone path to the house's wraparound porch. Kate assumed an official-looking stance and knocked on the door. Within seconds Ean Thornton appeared in the doorway. He frowned as his gaze flitted over Kate and the three officers behind her. "What do you want now, Kate?"

She held up the paper in her hand. "I have a warrant for Mike's arrest and another one to search your house, cars and any buildings on your property."

Ean's eyes grew wide and then clouded with dark anger. "Arrest? Have you lost your mind? You can't come into my house and arrest my son."

"Yes, I can, Ean. And if you don't stand aside and let us do our duty, we'll arrest you for obstruction of justice."

The man glared at Kate. His fists clenched at his sides, and he pulled his shoulders back as if he would stop anyone attempting to get past him. Austin stepped up beside Kate. "Mr. Thornton, we appreciate your feelings, but we will arrest you, too, if you interfere any further."

Ean's face turned crimson, and his eyes bulged. Kate took a step closer, and he slumped against the wall. "Then come in, but while you're searching, I'll be on the phone with my lawyer."

Brock watched as Kate and the officers disappeared into the house before he dropped down in a chair a few feet from the door. He wished he could be inside, but he really had no choice. He'd seen too much evidence thrown out by judges who ruled that search warrants had been violated.

An hour later the sound of the front door opening jerked him from the edge of sleep. He jumped to his feet and stared as Kate and Austin exited the house. Mike Thornton, his hands cuffed behind him, walked between them.

"No, you can't do this!" Ean's wail came from inside the house.

As the trio moved down the front steps, Ean ran from the house and stopped at the edge of the porch. Tears ran down his face. "Don't worry, son," he shouted. "I'll have you out of jail by tomorrow. My lawyer's already working on it."

The other agents walked from the house and stepped around Ean. They carried several boxes in their hands. Brock followed them and arrived at the cars just as Austin opened the back door of his car and motioned for Mike to get in. One of the agents handed Austin the box he held, climbed in beside Mike and shut the door. The other agent and Austin walked to the back of the car, popped the trunk and placed the boxes inside.

Brock turned to Kate. "What did you find in the house?"

"We found a gun in Mike's room, a laptop and several cameras that fit the description of stolen items. We'll send the gun to the lab in Raleigh to determine if it's the one that killed Jake, and we'll check the serial numbers of the items we found to see if they match the ones on our list. We also found a rifle in the trunk of Mike's car. Since we didn't find any shell casings at the beach, we can't prove it's the one used to shoot at Grady and me. I don't think that will be a problem because Calvin will testify that Mike told him he shot at us."

Brock gave a low whistle. "It sounds like you may have enough evidence for a conviction."

She nodded. "Yeah. I talked to Sheriff Baxter. He and one of the deputies are coming from the mainland on the emergency helicopter. They'll take Mike to the jail on Swan Quarter and collect the evidence."

He turned back to the car. "Then we'd better get going."

She walked to the driver's side of the car but stopped and stared over the top of the vehicle at the Thornton home before she opened the door. "Like I said, I always loved this house when I was growing up. It gleamed when the sun struck it, and I thought it looked like a place where a princess would live. It seemed so pure. Too bad that didn't reach to the family members living in it."

She shook her head and climbed into the car. Brock cast

one last look at the house before he joined her. He couldn't help but think how the beautiful home had hidden the answer to a man's murder and other crimes.

The person who had targeted Kate could be just like that. Maybe they saw him and talked with him every day and had no idea of the evil that lived inside him. His mouth went dry at the thought. Who was he and what motive did he have for tormenting Kate? The answers to those questions lay somewhere on Ocracoke, and they needed to find them before tragedy struck again.

Brock rubbed his eyes as the squad car stopped in front of Treasury's bed-and-breakfast. The clock on the cruiser's dial displayed a few minutes before eight.

By now Treasury had been up for hours, and the breakfast she would serve her guests sat on warmers in the dining room. The thought of her biscuits made Brock's stomach growl. He hoped he could stay awake long enough to eat.

Kate pushed the gearshift into Park and exhaled. "It's been a long night."

Brock had seen her tired at times since he'd been back, but he'd never seen her as drained of energy as she appeared this morning. He unfastened his seat belt and reached for the door handle. "You are going home to sleep, aren't you?"

She propped her elbows on the steering wheel, closed her eyes and massaged her temples. "I'm going to try. With everything that's happened, I may be too wired to sleep."

He released the door handle and settled back in his seat. "Last night had to be upsetting for you. It's never easy to arrest someone you've known for years, but I thought you handled Ean Thornton well."

She exhaled, and her shoulders slumped. "I knew he would be angry over the search warrant and wouldn't want to let us in his house, even though he really didn't have a choice. But

I didn't expect the change that came over him when we found that gun in Mike's room. I think for the first time Ean realized there was nothing he could do to make this go away."

Brock nodded. "I have to say I felt a little sorry for the guy when you were leading Mike to the car. I know it must be hard to see your son arrested."

Kate turned to stare at him. "I felt sorry for him, too, but then I got to thinking. If Ean had set some rules for Mike years ago, this might never have happened. I think Mike had gotten to the point he thought he could get away with anything."

Brock shook his head in disgust. "I see it all the time in my job, too. A young life wasted because he thought he was above the law. Now Mike doesn't have anything to look forward to but a lifetime of prison."

"If he's convicted."

"Don't worry. No jury is going to let him off. Not with the evidence you've put together." Brock opened the car door, stepped out and leaned down to stare into the car at her. "I'm glad Sheriff Baxter sent that deputy over to relieve you today. Now go home and get some sleep. I'll meet you back at the station at five this afternoon when you go back on patrol, and I'll ride with you all night."

She nodded and shifted into gear. "That sounds good. I'll see you there."

Brock stepped back onto the curb and watched as Kate's car disappeared down the street. He was about to walk toward the house when he spotted Dillon McAllister and Sam Burnett jogging toward him. Dillon ran about two paces in front of Sam, who seemed to be having trouble keeping up.

They came to a stop next to him. Perspiration poured down Sam's face, but Dillon's orange Tennessee Volunteers T-shirt and running shorts looked as if they'd just come from the laundry. Sam bent over, propped his hands on his knees and wheezed. Dillon grinned and jerked a finger in Sam's direction. "Sam and I went for a short run, but I think it's about done him in."

Sam straightened and glared at Dillon. "Short? I feel like we covered half of the island."

Dillon laughed and slapped Sam on the back. "Half of the island?" He rolled his eyes at Brock. "We ran to the Sandwich Shop and spent most of the time sitting in there and waiting for Sam to catch his breath."

Brock glanced from one to the other and chuckled. "Next time just tell him you'll meet him there, Sam."

"There won't be any next time with this guy," Sam muttered.

Brock tried to stifle a yawn, but he couldn't. He placed his hand over his mouth. "I've got to go, guys. I was up all night with Kate on patrol. I need to get some sleep."

Dillon nodded. "I can understand that. From what Grady said, it was a busy night."

Brock's eyes widened. "Where did you see Grady?"

"At the Sandwich Shop," Dillon said with a shrug. "There were a lot of island residents in there, and he was telling everybody about the police arresting some boy last night for that murder on the beach. He said the emergency helicopter came from the mainland a while ago and brought a deputy to cover for Kate today while she's getting some sleep."

Brock frowned and propped his hands on his hips. "What else did he say?"

"That they took the boy back in the helicopter to the jail over at Swan Quarter. He said something about the boy's father being upset."

Brock sighed. "Well, I guess the whole island knows by now about what happened last night."

"I expect you're right," Sam said. "The place was full of

people. So, Kate's gone home to sleep, but what about you? What are you going to do today?"

Brock yawned again. "I'm going to bed and sleep, I hope. Then I'll meet Kate late this afternoon to ride patrol with her again tonight." He glanced at his watch. "So I think I'll go upstairs and get in bed. Maybe I'll see you later today."

Brock turned and walked across the yard and onto the porch of the bed-and-breakfast. As he opened the door, he glanced over his shoulder at Sam and Dillon. He could hear Dillon trying to persuade Sam to take one more jog down to the end of the street and back. Sam shook his head and limped toward the front porch. Dillon laughed and trotted down the street.

Brock chuckled under his breath as he went inside and climbed the steps to his room. He stopped about halfway to the second floor and thought again about what the men had said about Grady talking to the crowd in the coffee shop.

By now the word was out that Jake Morgan's killer had turned out to be Mike Thornton, a kid who came from a family with deep roots on Ocracoke. All the time they had been so close to Jake's killer and didn't know it. The thought that they might also know Kate's adversary worried him.

Solving Jake's murder had reinforced something he'd learned as a rookie policeman. You can't overlook anyone in an investigation. Sometimes the one you least suspect turns out to be guilty in the end. That might hold true for the person who'd been terrorizing the island.

From now on, no one was above suspicion.

FIFTEEN

At five o'clock that afternoon Kate walked through the door of the police station. Her head thudded like a bass drum behind her aching eyes. She came to a halt as she entered and stared at Lisa behind the dispatch desk.

Lisa propped her elbow on the desk and tried to shield her eyes with her hand but not before Kate caught sight of the red eyes and swollen face. Kate eased across the floor and stopped beside her desk. She put a hand on Lisa's shoulder. "Are you all right?"

A wail escaped Lisa's mouth. She folded her arms on her desk and buried her face in them. "I can't believe it, Kate. Calvin, a thief and involved in Jake's murder."

Kate flatted her hand between Lisa's shoulder blades and rubbed in small circles. "I know," she crooned. "It's hard for me, too, but it's true. Calvin made his choices, and now he has to pay the price."

Lisa jerked her head up, and anger flashed in her eyes. "How could I have been so stupid? I thought he was the most wonderful man I'd ever met. I think I loved him, but I keep asking myself how I could have when he's nothing but a...but a..."

Kate nodded as Lisa searched for a word to describe Calvin. "He's a crook, Lisa, and you have to remember that.

He broke the law and violated the trust that the citizens of Ocracoke and the law enforcement community put in him. Keep that in mind."

Lisa pulled a tissue from a box on the corner of her desk and wiped at her eyes. "I'm trying, but it's so hard. Maybe in time."

Kate thought of how she'd been trying to forget Brock for the past six years, and she hadn't succeeded yet. She hoped Lisa had better luck than she had. She smiled. "We'll get through this, Lisa."

The ringing of the telephone on Lisa's desk startled Kate. Only nonemergency calls came in on that line, and Kate sighed. In the past few days she'd had to respond to more violent crime scenes than she would ever have believed. She could use a quiet call without any seriously injured victims.

Lisa grabbed the receiver. "Ocracoke Sheriff's Office. How may I help you?" She listened for a moment, scribbled something on a pad and nodded. "We'll have an officer there right away, sir."

When she hung up, Kate leaned over to see what she'd written. "What was that?"

Lisa handed her the paper she'd written on. "The man on the phone was calling to report a fender bender at the corner of Oyster Road and Forest Lane."

"Did he say who was involved in the accident?"

"No. He said it wasn't too bad, but he would need a police report for the insurance claim."

Kate turned and headed toward the door. "I'll go take this report and be right back. Brock is meeting me here. When he arrives, tell him where I've gone and that I'll be back as soon as I can."

"I'll take care of him. He'll probably bend my ear telling me how wonderful you are."

Lisa's words brought a smile to Kate's face as she exited

the station. For a long time, she had concentrated on Brock's faults, but the time she'd spent with him lately had opened her eyes to what a good person he really was.

Being with him again had stirred feelings in her that she thought would never surface again. The way he looked at her sometimes made her recall times in the past when he'd told her how beautiful she was and how she was what he had always dreamed of in a wife. Did he still think of her as a beautiful woman, or had she transformed into a tough law enforcement officer whose only appeal lay in her ability to overcome a fleeing suspect?

She unlocked the squad car, slid behind the wheel and buckled her seat belt. As she reached to turn the ignition, she glanced at the interior of the car. There was nothing feminine about her car. A shotgun hung on the rack of the backseat barrier behind her and a mobile data terminal sat between the driver's and passenger's seats. She had the latest technology at her fingertips, everything she could want in her job. But there was something missing—a man who loved her for the woman, not the deputy, she was.

She had thought for years nothing mattered but her job and caring for her sisters. That had become her life. Although she loved her sisters and her job with all her heart, she needed more. Brock had come back, and the part of her heart that had insisted she could never love again had been proven wrong.

Tears filled her eyes. She couldn't deny the truth anymore. She loved Brock. In fact she had never quit loving him, but it would do her no good. He would leave soon and go back to his life, and she would be left with the existence she'd made for herself on her island.

Gritting her teeth, she cranked the car and drove toward the spot where the fender bender had been reported. Kate knew the intersection well. It wasn't too far from her home.

She drove through the village along the road that ran the

length of the island. It only took a few minutes before she spotted the turnoff onto Oyster Road. She guided the squad car onto the gravel road and drove along it. In the distance she spotted a car parked at the spot where Forest Lane intersected the road.

As Kate pulled to a stop, she saw only one car. Not two. Lisa hadn't said this was a hit-and-run, but it must have been. She stepped out of the car and looked around. A man bent down as if looking at the front bumper. The hood of the car blocked her view of his face.

"Hello," she said. "I'm here in response to a call about a fender bender."

"Thanks for coming. I made the call." The man didn't straighten and face her.

With an instinct forged from her years in the sheriff's department, Kate touched the gun at her waist, took a step and squinted at the figure. The car's hood hid his face, but she could see the orange T-shirt pulled tight across his back. "Can you tell me what happened?"

"Yes, I can." The man took a deep breath before he rose to his full height and turned to face her.

Kate gasped, and her hand dropped to her side. She took a step back before she recovered from the surprise of facing Dillon McAllister. She arched an eyebrow and pointed to his T-shirt. "A teacher at the University of Arkansas wearing the Tennessee logo? What would your bosses think?"

He smiled. "They wouldn't mind. They're Tennessee fans, too."

He stood there in his running shorts and T-shirt, muscles tensed, looking as if he might take off on a jog at any minute. Her skin tingled as the icy inkling she'd experienced before rippled up and down her spine. She wiggled her shoulders and glanced up and down the road. "What are you doing way out here?"

He held one hand behind his back as he walked around the car. "Waiting for you."

The tone of his voice and the gleam in his eye set off a warning in Kate's mind. Something wasn't right. She glanced up and down the road again. "Where is the car that hit you?"

He narrowed his eyes and stepped closer. "There wasn't another car, Kate."

Danger. Danger. The word flashed through her mind like a blinking sign. She eased a step backward. "I don't understand." She reached down and placed her hand on the grip of the gun in her holster again.

His gaze flicked over her hand and back to her face. "I wouldn't do that if I were you, Kate."

She tightened her hold on the pistol to pull it out, but she was too late. He jerked his hand from behind his back and pulled the trigger of the Taser gun he held. Electrical shock waves pulsed through Kate's body. She tumbled to the ground in a trembling heap. Paralyzing impulses surged through her body. Her mind told her to move, but her muscles refused to respond.

Dillon leaned over her, took her gun and handcuffs from her belt, and flipped her facedown in the road. Kate felt the cuffs snap around her wrists, but she could only lie stunned and helpless in the dirt.

She heard the door of Dillon's car opening, and then he bent down with his mouth next to her ear. "When I woke up this morning, I knew the time was right. So here we are. The one thing I want to accomplish today is to *Live and Let Die.*"

The words echoed in her pounding head and sent fear racing through her body. At last she knew the identity of the person who wanted her dead. The answer to why she had no idea.

He grabbed her by the arm and dragged her to her feet.

Kate's legs wobbled like limp spaghetti, and she sagged against him. He laughed, shoved her into the backseat of his car and slammed the door.

Even with her head still vibrating from the electrical pulses, Kate knew when he climbed in the car and started the engine. Then they were moving. Where was he taking her? She tried to wiggle her arms, but they wouldn't respond.

She took a deep breath and willed herself to be still. The effects of the Taser would wear off in a few minutes. All she had to do was wait and watch for her opportunity to attack Dillon.

They drove a short distance and stopped. Fear choked her throat. Had he driven her to a lonely place to kill her? The back door of the car opened, and he jerked her from the car and into a standing position next to him.

Her wobbly legs threatened to collapse, and the fear she'd felt a moment ago escalated into full-blown horror when she saw where she stood—facing her own house. At this time of day her sisters would be inside. Panic swept through her. Her knees buckled, but his hand gripped her arm and steadied her.

"Why, Dillon? I'd never seen you before last week. Why do you want to hurt me?" The forced words ripped at her parched throat.

He laughed and gouged her in the back with her own hand-gun. "You'll know before long. Now let's go meet your sisters."

Some feeling had returned to her legs. She tried to dig her feet into the sandy soil, but it was no use. The black bag that hung on his shoulder jostled as he pushed her forward and propelled her up the front steps. Opening the front door, he nudged her into the living room and closed the door behind him.

"Anybody home?" he called out.

Footsteps from the kitchen made Kate's heart almost stop. Betsy, a dish towel in her hands, appeared in the doorway. Emma ran from the kitchen and darted around Betsy. Emma's face broke into a big smile. "Hi, Mr. McAllister. What are you doing here?"

Emma started toward Dillon, but Kate took a step forward to block her way. "No, Emma. Stay back."

At Kate's sharp words, Betsy reached out, grabbed Emma and pulled her backward. Her forehead wrinkled, and she wrapped her arms around the child. "Kate, what's going on?"

Dillon pulled the gun from Kate's back and pointed it at Emma. "I'm here for a short visit, and you need to do whatever I ask or I'll shoot your sister."

Betsy's face paled, and her mouth dropped open. The dish towel in her hand drifted to the floor. She hugged Emma tighter.

Kate's heart pumped. She tried to kick at Dillon, but he avoided the blow and laughed. He ran the barrel of the gun down Kate's cheek and pushed her a step closer to her sisters but didn't let go of her arm. He tossed the bag that still hung on his shoulder to Betsy and narrowed his eyes. "This is what I want you to do. Look in the bag and take out the roll of electrical tape you'll find. Then put the bag on the floor. I want you to take Emma in the bedroom, wrap her feet together tightly, her arms behind her back and a piece of tape across her mouth. If you leave the tape loose, I will shoot Kate. Do you understand?"

Betsy nodded and glanced at Kate before she did as he said. When she had the tape in hand, she led Emma to the bedroom. Dillon guided Kate to the door, and they watched as Betsy followed his orders. When she'd finished, she looked up. Tears rolled down her face. "All right. I've done what you said."

He took a step backward. "Good. Now let's go to the kitchen."

Kate glanced at Emma, and her heart shattered at the fear in the child's eyes. "Don't worry, Emma. Everything's going to be all right."

Emma's wild-eyed stare jerked from Betsy to Kate. Nausea rumbled in Kate's stomach. Betsy smiled through her tears and kissed the child on the face. "Kate's right. You stay here. We'll be back."

In the kitchen, Dillon hooked his foot underneath a chair at the table and pulled it into the middle of the floor. He positioned Kate in front of it, slid her arms over the back and pushed her into the chair before he looked back at Betsy. "Now do the same with Kate. I'll be watching, and if you don't make it tight, I'll shoot Emma. Right now she's a sitting duck."

Betsy dropped to her knees and began to wrap the tape around Kate. "I'm so sorry, Betsy," Kate whispered. "I have no idea why he's doing this. I wish I could have spared you and Emma from being involved."

Betsy looked up at Kate. Her lips trembled. "It's all right, Kate. We're a family, and we'll face this together." She pulled a piece of tape off and positioned it in front of her mouth. "I love you, Kate."

"I love you, too. Tell Emma I love her."

Muffling a sob, Betsy pressed the tape to Kate's mouth.

Dillon grabbed Betsy by the arm and pulled her to her feet. "Now it's your turn."

Kate turned her head to get a glimpse as Dillon propelled her out of the room. She strained to hear what was happening. Tape was ripped from the roll with a sharp crackle, the sound drifting into the room. After a moment a bed creaked. He had tied Betsy up and made her lie down beside Emma. Now all three of them were helpless.

She had to do something. Glancing around the kitchen, she searched for something that would help her loosen her bonds. A knife lay on the counter across the room. Could she get to it before Dillon returned? She tensed her body and jerked upward with all her might. The chair rose and thudded back to the floor less than an inch from its original spot.

Rascal's low growl reached Kate's ear. Where was he? Her gaze darted about the room and came to rest on the door that led to the utility room just off the kitchen. Emma must have sneaked the cat inside when Betsy wasn't looking, and now he probably lay in his favorite spot—in a basket of dirty laundry.

Thoughts of Rascal vanished as Dillon ambled back into the kitchen. He tossed the tape on the table and placed his hand over his mouth to stifle a yawn. He spotted the full coffeepot on the kitchen counter and pulled a mug from the cabinet. After he poured himself some coffee, he sat down at the kitchen table, took a sip and smiled. "It's been a long day, and that tastes good. I'll have to tell Betsy she makes good coffee."

Kate glared at him. How she wished she could rip the tape from her mouth and tell him how despicable he was. He set his mug down and laughed. "You're wondering about me, aren't you, Kate? Well, I guess I should set your mind at ease about some things. As smart as you are, I know you've already figured out that I'm the man you've been looking for. The only thing you don't know is why I've targeted you."

He got up and walked toward her. She didn't flinch as he leaned over her. He brought his face close to hers. "You act tough, Kate, but I know inside you're scared. What am I going to do to you and your sisters? You'll have to wait a little longer to find out that." He smiled, reached down and pulled her cell phone from its clip.

Walking back to the table, he sat down in the chair and laid the cell phone on the table in front of him. He took another sip of coffee, laced his fingers behind his head and leaned back in his chair. "Now we wait for your boyfriend to call."

SIXTEEN

Brock yanked his shoelaces into a knot and scowled. He hadn't meant to sleep so long, but Treasury had insisted he stay up until she'd served breakfast. While they ate, Treasury had begged him to tell everybody about the latest developments in Jake's murder case. It had been several hours before he'd been able to get to bed. With the curtains drawn and the room so cool, he'd dropped right off and hadn't stirred.

He glanced at his watch and groaned. It was already five o'clock, and Kate had probably arrived at the station by now. He needed to call and let her know he was running late. His cell phone lay on the dresser across the room, and he hurried toward it.

Before he reached it, his favorite country music song vibrated in the quiet room—the ring tone for Don Bennett. His heart skipped a beat. There was only one reason the private investigator would be calling him. Kate's brother.

Brock pulled the phone from the charger and jammed it against his ear. "Hey, Don. I'm surprised to hear from you so soon."

A chuckle sounded on the phone. "You shouldn't be. Don't you know by now that I don't mess around when I have a case? I get right on it."

Brock swallowed and closed his eyes. "Then you must have some news for me. Have you found Scott Michaels?"

"I have. He's sitting right here with me."

"And where is that?"

"San Antonio."

Relief surged through Brock. "Does he live there?"

Don hesitated for a moment before he spoke. "No. He's been in the hospital here."

Brock's relief melted. Concern laced Don's words and sent goose bumps racing up Brock's back. "What's the matter with him?"

Don took a deep breath. "Let me get Scott on the phone. He can tell you."

There was silence for a moment before a man's soft voice spoke. "Mr. Gentry, this is Scott Michaels. Mr. Bennett tells me you're a friend of my sisters'." He paused for a moment. "*My sisters*. I can't believe I'm saying those words."

Brock sucked in his breath. There was something about the man's voice that reminded him of Kate. "Yes. I'm here on Ocracoke with all three of them—Kate, Betsy and Emma."

"This is the best news I've ever had. I've wondered all these years if I had family out there, but my aunt always told me my parents were killed when I was a baby. She never told me anything about where my father came from or if he had any family."

"And you never asked?"

"I did when I was a child, but she convinced me that we only had each other. She died a few years ago, and now I find out she'd kept my father from me."

"Your sisters found out about you, and they've been searching for years. They want to meet you and be a part of your life if you want that. Would you like to come to Ocracoke to meet them?"

He hesitated. "When Mr. Bennett told me I have three

sisters, it was the happiest moment of my life. I thought I was alone in the world, and now I find out I have family." He paused a moment. "I want to meet them more than anything, but they may change their minds about being a part of my life when they find out more about me."

Brock's eyebrows arched. "Why?"

Scott exhaled, and in it Brock detected an offer of rejection. "I'm not well, Mr. Gentry. I've been a soldier for the past ten years. I've spent time in places that most people have never heard of, and I've done things in battle that have left invisible but very real injuries to my mind and body. I've experienced a lot of horrors that have left me suffering from PTSD— post-traumatic stress disorder. Right now I'm in a research program at Brooke Army Medical Center in San Antonio. I still have a lot of problems that my sisters may not want to deal with."

Brock hesitated. What should he say? If Scott had demons in his life he was facing, it might be better for Kate and her sisters not to meet him. Then he remembered how Kate had talked about her brother and how part of their family was missing. He also thought of her faith and how she placed everything in God's hands. She had been teaching him that ever since he came to Ocracoke, and that same belief had slowly taken root in his heart.

He smiled. He knew what he had to say.

"Scott, your sisters want to meet you. They have a deep faith in God, and they'll help you work through your problems."

A soft gasp tickled Brock's ear. "They're believers, too? This is more wonderful than I could have imagined. Then I'm coming to Ocracoke." He chuckled. "It's a funny thing, you know. I'd never heard of Ocracoke Island, but something about the name sounds like home. Tell my sisters that Mr. Bennett and I are taking a plane out in the morning.

When we get to Raleigh, we'll rent a car and drive to Swan Quarter. We've checked the ferry schedules, so we should arrive late tomorrow afternoon."

"Good. I'm on my way to see Kate right now. They're going to be so happy to get this news. By the way, when you board the ferry, have Don call me so we can meet you when you arrive."

"I'll do that, and thank you, Mr. Gentry. I appreciate what you've done for me."

"I'm glad Don was able to find you. We'll see you tomorrow."

Brock closed the phone and gripped it in his hand. Should he call Kate and tell her the good news? He shook his head. This deserved to be delivered in person so he could see her face when he told her.

He rushed from the room, down the stairs and out to the car. Within minutes he was on his way to the police station. He pulled to a stop in the station's parking lot and glanced around. Kate's car was nowhere in sight. Maybe she hadn't made it to work yet.

Smiling, he raced to the porch and through the front door. Lisa sat at her desk, her attention directed to her computer screen. Austin Whitman, holding the day's newspaper, lounged in a chair across the room.

Lisa stood up from her desk and stretched her arms over her head. "Hi, Brock."

Brock glanced around. "Where's Kate?"

"We had a call about a fender bender. She left to take the report. She should be back any minute."

Brock nodded and ambled across the room to where Austin sat. He dropped down in a chair beside him. "Did the paper get the news about Mike Thornton's arrest in this edition?"

Austin pushed up straighter in his chair. "They did. Want to read it?" He passed the newspaper over to Brock.

"Thanks."

Brock read the article, then rifled through the rest of the paper. Most of the news on the island revolved around events and activities that would interest tourists. After a few minutes he'd scanned it from front to back.

He handed the paper back to Austin and glanced at his watch. Standing, he crossed the room to Lisa's desk. "How long ago did Kate leave on that call?"

Lisa looked up at the clock on the wall and frowned. "About thirty minutes. She should have been back by now." She reached for the radio mic. "Do you want me to see if I can reach her?"

Brock's stomach fluttered, and a bitter taste flooded his mouth. He grimaced. "Yes."

Lisa pulled the mic to her mouth. "One-one-seven, come in." No answer. Lisa frowned. "One-one-seven, come in." Still no answer. Lisa glanced up, a frown wrinkling her forehead. "I don't understand why she's not answering."

"Let me try her cell phone." Brock pulled out his phone and punched in her number. It rang several times before he heard the connection, but Kate didn't answer. "Kate." No answer. "Kate! Are you there?"

"Kate's tied up right now and can't come to the phone."

The words trickled through his body like ice water pouring from his head to his toes. He gripped the edge of Lisa's desk with his free hand and tightened his hold on the phone with the other. "Who is this?"

A laugh rumbled in Brock's ear. "Someone you know well, Brock. I've had a lot of fun on this island. First it was the deputy, then the fire at the theater and the big explosion. Oh, that was beautiful."

Brock gasped at the cruel tone of the caller's voice. "Are you telling me that you're the one responsible for the murder of four innocent people?"

A shrill laugh pierced Brock's ear. "Guilty."

A chair scraped across the floor, and Austin Whitman hurried to stand beside Brock. "Is that our killer?" Austin whispered.

Brock nodded and glanced at Lisa, whose face had turned white. Brock took a deep breath. "Let me talk to Kate."

"I told you she's tied up, and I mean that literally. Right along with her two sisters."

Terror kicked him in the stomach. "Wh-what do you want?"

"I want you, Brock," the caller snapped. "I want you to come to Kate's house alone. If you bring anyone with you, I'll kill Kate and her two sisters. Do you understand?"

"Why are you doing this?" Brock yelled.

"Come to Kate's house alone, and you'll find out. When you get here, come in the front door and walk to the kitchen. You'll find us there."

The call disconnected with a click that left Brock in stunned silence. Austin grabbed him by the arm. "What did he say?"

Brock closed his eyes and swallowed the fear that rose in his throat. "He's holding Kate, Betsy and Emma prisoner at their house. He says he'll kill them if I don't come alone."

Lisa jammed her fist in her mouth and glanced from Brock to Austin.

Austin pulled out his gun and checked it before replacing it in his holster. "Well, one thing's for sure. You're not going alone."

Brock held up his hands in protest and backed away. "No, you can't go. He said he'll kill them."

"But he'll kill you, too, Brock."

Brock shook his head. "No, I can't risk getting them all killed."

Austin glared at him. "Think like a police officer, not

Kate's friend. You can't help her if you go alone. Maybe between the two of us, we can get this guy before he kills them."

Lisa rose from behind her desk and stared at him. "Austin's right, Brock. Kate wouldn't want you to go in there without backup. She would have faith that you would respond like the trained officer you are."

There was that word again. *Faith*. Even now he knew Kate had faith that God was in control. The strange thing was that he believed it, too. Kate had shown him the way to a faith that would overcome the guilt he'd held onto, and now it would help him face whatever happened at her house. He glanced from Lisa to Austin.

"Okay, Austin. Let's go see if we can put an end to this crazy killer's rampage on Ocracoke."

Kate struggled not to let her eyes betray the fear that crept through her as Dillon closed her cell phone. He replaced the phone on the kitchen table and laughed. Smiling, he walked behind the chair where she was held prisoner and bent down with his mouth next to her ear. His warm breath sent chills up and down her spine.

"I suppose you heard. Your boyfriend will be here any-time now. All of my plans and my actions have led up to that moment. It won't be long now, Kate. You'll know soon."

His taunting voice grated on every nerve ending in her body. Her eyes blinked, and she widened them in hopes that he hadn't noticed that one flicker of fear.

She cringed as he placed his hands on her shoulders and gently caressed them. "You're a very beautiful woman, Kate. I don't blame Brock for caring about you so much. I used to love someone, too, but she left."

Kate wiggled her shoulders in an attempt to escape his hold, but he laughed and inched his fingers up to her neck.

She wondered if the pulse in her neck echoed the erratic cadence of her heartbeat as his touch moved upward until he stopped with his fingers on either side of her mouth.

Kate stiffened as his left hand slowly stroked her cheek. His thumb and index finger grabbed the edge of the tape covering her mouth. Pain exploded in her head at the violent jerk that pulled the tape from her mouth.

He laughed and walked around the chair to face her. "Is that more comfortable?"

Kate rubbed her lips together to stem the tingling pain before she spoke. She tilted her head to stare up at him. "Why, Dillon? That's what I want to know. What did I ever do to you?"

His eyes grew wide. "Why nothing, Kate. You've been very friendly to me ever since I've been on the island. You were just the bait I needed to get who I'm really after."

She frowned. "You've killed four people, another is in critical condition and you've terrorized a packed theater for what? To use me as bait? I don't understand."

He crossed his arms and smirked. "You're smarter than that, Kate. Who do you think?"

She shook her head. "I have no—" She stopped midsentence as understanding reared its head in her mind. Her eyes grew wide at the reality of what she'd just heard. She did know who he was after, and she could hardly speak his name. "Brock?" she whispered.

Dillon laughed and pointed a finger at her. "Bingo! You win the prize. And let me show it to you."

He turned to the table where the black bag he'd brought with him lay and unzipped it. He reached inside and pulled out a hypodermic needle and held it up. A clear liquid filled the syringe. The way Dillon held it toward her told Kate some sinister plan was about to unfold.

"Wh-what's that for?"

Dillon's face hardened into an angry mask, and he gritted his teeth. "Never mind. Just do as I say, and everything will be fine. When your boyfriend gets here, I want you to call him into the kitchen. Then I'll take it from there."

Kate shook her head. "I won't help you kill Brock."

An angry snort rumbled from Dillon's mouth. "You'd better be worried about your two sisters in the bedroom. Do you want them to live? The way I see it, Kate. You have a choice. Brock or your sisters. Think about that until he gets here. Now I'm not talking anymore."

Dillon sank down in the chair where he'd sat earlier and trained his attention toward the door into the kitchen where Brock would have to enter. Kate studied his body language. He sat straight with every muscle tensed. He looked like an animal ready to pounce for the kill.

He had said she had to choose who would die, but she knew the truth. Dillon had gone to great lengths to plan his attack on Brock, and he had left Ocracoke littered with bodies on his quest. At this point a few more didn't matter.

The sick feeling in the pit of her stomach told Kate that Dillon didn't want just Brock. There was no way he'd leave three witnesses. When Dillon left, she, Brock and her two sisters would all be dead.

SEVENTEEN

Brock stopped the car on the island's main road at the turn-off to Kate's house. He glanced in the rearview mirror and watched the car carrying the two ATF agents pull to a stop behind him. Austin had insisted they come as backup. The agreement was, however, that the two men would approach the house only if Austin summoned them.

Brock gripped the steering wheel and turned his head to stare at Austin. "The house is down this road. I'm going to let you out here. You can work your way down the beach and come up over the dune ridge to the back door. He said they were in the kitchen. There's a small window over the sink. Maybe you can see in and know what's happening."

Austin nodded. "Does the back door open into the kitchen?"

"No. It opens into a small utility room. Unless they've re-modeled, it's a narrow room with a washer and dryer on one side and a closet and sink on the other."

Austin pursed his lips and stared through the windshield. "I don't have to tell you that we're dealing an unstable character. He's killed four people already and one or two more probably won't bother him at all."

"I know."

Austin took a deep breath and grabbed the door handle. "Be careful, Gentry."

"You, too, Whitman."

The agent crouched low and ran toward the dune that skirted the road. When he'd disappeared onto the beach, Brock glanced in the rearview mirror again, waved to the agents behind and put the car in gear. He eased down on the accelerator, and the car inched forward. As he approached the house, his heartbeat increased until his tight chest felt as if it would burst.

He'd been here many times in the past, but never on a life-or-death mission like now. The last time he'd come had been the night of Doug's death. He and Kate had sat on the beach, and she had talked to him of her faith in God. He'd come a long way in his journey toward finding God since then, but there were things he still questioned. Kate believed God always walked with you wherever you went. He wanted to believe God was with him right now. But was He?

Brock stopped the car in the house's front yard and dropped his head to rest on his hands that gripped the steering wheel. He felt so alone. He'd been in dangerous situations before, but he'd never experienced one like this. A madman held captive the woman he loved and her two sisters. Only he and Austin could put a stop to their almost certain death. And they needed some divine intervention if they were to succeed.

If God was with him, Brock needed to know now. His lips began to move in silent prayer. *God, I feel so alone, but I have to help Kate and her sisters. Don't let them die. Please don't bring them this far in finding their brother to have it all be for nothing. All I want is to know You're watching over us. Kate believes it. Just show me. Please show me.*

He didn't move but sat still, waiting for the revelation of God's presence he needed. He didn't know how God would speak to him, but if He was real, He'd do something. Brock waited, but nothing happened.

The heavens didn't open to reveal a blinding light that

carried the voice of God to earth. Nor did his heart fill with wonder at God's message spilling into his soul. There was nothing. He groaned and shook his head. Nothing. No assurance whatsoever that anyone or anything watched him. Why had he thought God could love a person like him—one who had broken the heart of the only woman he'd ever loved, hated his father for years and been the cause of an innocent man's death?

He opened the car door and stepped out. He squared his shoulders and took a faltering step toward the house. He placed his foot on the first of the front porch steps and froze. A distant cry reached his ears. He turned his head to stare toward the sun that was slowly sinking in the west, and he heard it again. The call of a Black-crowned Night Heron.

His skin warmed from the blood that pounded in his veins. He remembered the night he and Kate sat on the beach and she'd told him how she heard God's voice in all the sounds of Ocracoke. They'd heard a Black-crowned Night Heron that night. Kate said dusk was their feeding time, the time when she could hear God's voice in their call. The sound of the bird's cry drifted over the dunes once again, and Brock knew the prayer he'd whispered in the car had just been answered.

God had spoken to him in the voice of a bird, and His message that He controlled the situation inside the house pierced Brock's heart. God did care about what happened to His children.

Tears filled Brock's eyes, and he stared upward. He wasn't alone. This was God's battle, not his and not Austin's. They were there merely as God's messengers, and whatever happened, God was in control.

A new strength flowed through him, and he mounted the steps with an assurance he had never felt before. On the porch he gripped the doorknob, pushed the door open and stepped into the living room. His footsteps echoed on the hardwood floor as he walked forward.

He stopped in the middle of the living room and glanced around. A dish towel lay on the floor in the doorway that led to the kitchen. Nothing else appeared out of place. He took a deep breath and eased forward.

"Kate. Are you in here?"

Her voice drifted from the back of the house. "We're in the kitchen, Brock. Be careful. He has a gun."

"I'm coming in," he called out. He held his hands in front of him as he eased around the door into the kitchen. "I'm unarmed."

The scene inside the kitchen hit him like a jolt of electricity. The horror of seeing Kate tied in a chair gave way to surprise at Dillon McAllister, dressed in the same running shorts and T-shirt he'd worn earlier today, standing behind her with a gun to her head. The sight of a hypodermic needle lying on the table beside Kate's chair sent chills up his spine.

Dillon smiled. "We've been waiting for you, Brock."

Brock shook his head in disbelief. Dillon? A murderer? It wasn't possible that the person who had taunted Kate and killed four people could be the man who'd occupied a room next to his at the Island Connection. Not the man he'd laughed and talked with for the past week. He took a step closer. "D-Dillon," he sputtered. "I don't understand. Why are you doing this to Kate?"

Dillon sighed. "I've already told Kate. It's not about her, Brock. I like Kate a lot. She just has the wrong friends."

The answer made no sense. "Wrong friends? But how could you know any of her friends? You told us you'd never been to Ocracoke, that you were a college professor here to study the island's history. Was that a lie?"

"I'm afraid so. I've never been so bored in my life as I was traipsing through all those salt marshes while Grady rattled on about his famous ancestor."

Brock raked his fingers through his hair. "This is crazy. Why did you go to so much trouble because you say Kate has the wrong friends?"

Dillon rolled his eyes. "Brock, don't you get it? I only used Kate to get to the one person that I hate more than anyone else I've ever known."

"Who?"

Dillon's eyes darkened, and pure hatred lined his face. "You."

Brock gasped and drew back in surprise. "Me? I never saw you before you showed up at Treasury's bed-and-breakfast."

"I know. And I only came there because I knew that was where you were planning to stay." Dillon smiled. "You see, Brock, I've had a private investigator following your every move for months. When he found out you were taking some time off, he went to your partner's favorite hangout and bought him a drink. One thing led to another and before the night was over, your friend and partner was so drunk he never remembered talking about how you were going to Ocracoke Island to try and make amends with the only woman you've ever loved. He even knew the name of the bed-and-breakfast." He nudged Kate on the shoulder with the gun. "I guess it's true what they say. Police officers share everything with their partners."

Kate's face hadn't shown any reaction to Dillon's words the whole time he spoke. Brock licked his lips and moved closer. "What did I ever do to you, Dillon?"

His features hardened, and a snarl erupted from his lips. "Maybe I need to introduce myself. My name isn't Dillon McAllister. It's Robert Sterling Jr."

The name slammed into Brock's head like a freight train, and he reeled. "You're Sterling's son?"

"Yes."

Kate frowned and twisted her head to stare at Dillon, then looked back at Brock. "His father was the man who was executed?"

Brock nodded. "Yes."

Dillon pressed the gun tighter against Kate's head. Brock's skin burned from the hatred raging in Dillon's eyes. "Can you even start to imagine what it was like for my father on death row all those years for a crime he didn't commit? Then to be executed when you knew the truth?" He glared at Brock. "You could have saved him, but you didn't."

Dillon's eyes blinked several times before his gaze darted about the room. His hand shook, and Brock feared he might discharge the pistol at any moment. He had to keep Dillon distracted from the gun. He needed to keep him talking long enough to give Austin time to get to the back of the house. "I didn't know he was innocent, Dillon."

"Call me Robert!" The shouted words rattled against the walls.

Brock licked his lips. "All right, Robert. I left a message for my partner to check out the man's story. He never saw it. I'm sorry your father died. It was a horrible mix-up."

"Mix-up?" he roared. The gun dangled in Robert's limp hand. "It can't be undone. My father died an agonizing death by lethal injection, and you call it a mix-up? Well, how about another one." He reached for the syringe on the table.

Brock's blood chilled when he saw that the protective cap had already been removed. The needle gleamed in the light from the ceiling fixture. Brock held his hand up and inched forward. "I don't understand, Robert. How did you pull off everything you did on the island? For instance, Doug's death."

Robert laughed. "If you remember, I was supposed to meet Grady at ten that morning. I'd followed that deputy for a few days and knew what his early morning schedule was like. I beat him to the Pirate Creek Road that morning and pretended to have car trouble. When he stopped to help, I killed him."

Kate's eyes blazed with anger. She sucked in her breath. "How about the night of the play? I saw you with Sam and Tracey. How did you manage that?"

Robert shrugged. "That was no problem. I had another pirate costume in my car that was parked nearby. I changed and was back to the festival before you were through looking at Brock's injuries."

Brock inched closer to Robert. "What about the notes? Why did you use song titles?"

"That was in honor of my father. While he sat in isolation on death row in a cell about the size of a walk-in closet, his only contact with the outside world was from the small radio the prison authorities let him have. He spent hours listening to music, most of it the oldies. It was like he was reliving his life again."

"I know that must have been hard." Brock licked at his lips. "But I don't think your father would have wanted you to hurt innocent people. Don't hurt another one. Kate has done nothing to deserve what you've planned for her."

Robert glanced down at Kate. His body tensed. "What about the way I've suffered? I couldn't help my father, and now you can't help Kate. I want you to hurt like I did when my father was killed. An eye for an eye, so to speak."

The sight of Dillon's thumb on the plunger paralyzed Brock, and he gasped. "Be careful, Robert. I'm begging you not to hurt Kate."

Robert laughed and moved the needle closer to the vein in Kate's neck. "Just one little prick, and it will be all over."

"No!" Brock cried. "Let Kate and her sisters go, and take me, instead. After all, it's me you hate, not them."

Robert's wild laugh pierced Brock's ears. Robert shook his

head. "Do you really love her so much that you'd give your life for her?"

Brock dropped his gaze to Kate's face and let it wander over her. In that moment the past six years washed away, and he saw them as they were then, a couple who loved each other with a deep passion. It had never changed for him.

He nodded. "I do. I love her so much I would willingly give my life for hers."

Robert chuckled and leaned toward Kate. "Isn't that touching? He loves you, Kate." He straightened and stared at Brock. "I loved a woman, too, but she left me when my father was executed. She said I had become too obsessed with revenge. So you see, Brock, you not only took my father from me, but you drove my wife away, too." His eyes hardened. "You've got to pay for that."

Brock glanced at the window and caught a brief glimpse of Austin's face before he disappeared from view. He had to keep Robert occupied. He moved closer to the table. *Keep his mind on me instead of Kate,* Brock thought.

Brock eased closer. "Let's talk about this, Robert. You don't want to hurt Kate. You really want me. Isn't there some way we could work out a trade?"

Robert shook his head. "No trade. My father died by lethal injection, and you're going to watch Kate die that way, too." He smiled down at Kate. "Don't worry. Yours will be over much quicker than my father's was."

Robert touched the needle to Kate's skin. She clamped her lips closed but made no sound.

"Stop!" The word sprang from Brock's lips. "Don't do this. I beg you not to hurt Kate."

Robert hesitated and pulled the syringe back. "You beg me?" he scoffed. "Where was justice when my father begged for it?" His gaze raked Brock. "You really do love her, don't you?"

"I do. Please don't hurt her. Let her and her sisters go, and I'll take their place. After all, I'm the one you want."

Robert narrowed his eyes and stared at Brock. "I'm sorry I can't oblige you today. I decided before I ever came here that Kate was going to die so you would know what it's like to lose someone you love." He darted a glance toward the bedroom. "But you don't think I'd leave any witnesses, do you? Kate goes first, then you and finally the sisters who are lying tied up on the bed."

Kate's leg twitched. Brock suspected she'd begun to lose the control she'd always had over her emotions with the mention of her sisters. He had no doubt that she would willingly give her life to save Betsy and Emma, but at the moment she was helpless.

A choking sob rattled in Kate's throat. "Please don't hurt my sisters. Emma's just a child."

Robert shook his head. "Sorry, Kate."

Brock clenched his fists and took a step toward Kate but stopped when Robert held up the syringe. Robert shook his head. "It's time to tell Kate goodbye."

Panic sliced through Brock's heart. "I'm sorry, Kate. I'm sorry. I never should have led him here."

Her lips trembled, and a tear slid from the corner of her eye. "It's all right, Brock. Remember what I said about who controls my life."

God, where are You? Brock's mind screamed.

A splintering crash at the back door followed by a high-pitched screech shattered the quiet room. Robert whirled toward the utility room just as a gray ball of fur dashed toward him. Shrieking in the most unearthly voice Brock had ever heard, Rascal jumped over Robert's feet and clawed at the floor for a footing as he skidded behind him.

With a startled cry Robert stumbled backward and landed

on Rascal's tail, which only enraged the cat more. He leaped up and clawed at Robert's bare legs.

Brock lunged forward as Robert tried to kick free of the cat. Locking a grip around both of Robert's wrists, Brock plowed his full weight into his chest. Robert's breath fanned Brock's ear, and he pushed harder until Robert stood pinned against the kitchen sink.

Austin Whitman, his gun drawn, appeared in the utility room door, sprinted across the kitchen floor and grabbed Robert's left arm in a death grip. As he exerted pressure, the hand holding the gun opened, and the weapon dropped to the floor.

Robert fought like a cornered animal and struggled against Brock's grip on the hand that held the syringe. Austin shoved his gun under Robert's chin. "Drop the syringe."

Robert twisted in one last attempt to escape, but he was no match for the two men holding him. He took his thumb off the plunger and loosened his grip. Brock reached up, pulled the syringe from Robert's hand and laid it on the counter next to the sink.

Together Brock and Austin pinned Robert facedown on the floor. They had just slipped handcuffs on him when Brock heard footsteps running across the living room floor. The two backup agents appeared at the kitchen door. "Is everybody all right?"

Brock nodded toward the bedroom. "There's a woman and a child tied up in there. Check on them."

One of the agents hurried out of the room, and the other helped Austin pull Robert to his feet. Still on the floor, Brock raked his trembling fingers through his hair. Glancing up at Austin, he struggled to calm his racing heart. "I almost had a heart attack when that door crashed open and Rascal ran through here."

A sheepish grin lined Austin's mouth. "The door was

locked. I didn't have any other choice than to kick it in. When that cat jumped out of the laundry basket, it scared me so badly that I almost fell back out the door."

Brock pushed to his feet. "The commotion diverted Sterling just long enough for me to rush him." He came around the chair to face Kate. Her lips trembled, but she didn't speak. He realized she hadn't spoken since the struggle. He dropped to his knees and cupped her cheek in his hand. "Are you all right?"

She nodded and blinked back the tears he could see in her eyes. "I'm fine, thanks to you and Austin." She glanced at Robert, who stood between the two ATF agents then back to Brock. "Will you cut this tape off me?"

He'd expected her to say something more personal. Especially after he'd bared his heart in front of her. No matter what she said, though, he was just happy she was alive. He rose. "Sure."

When she was free and able to stand, Kate turned to the agents who still held Robert. She clenched her fists and stared into the man's face. "You killed Doug O'Neil, a young man who only wanted to be a good police officer, and Russell and Rose Johnson, two of the nicest people I've ever known, and a man who just happened to deliver fireworks to Ocracoke. Then you threatened everybody I love. How could you be so cruel?"

Robert glared at her but didn't answer.

Agent Whitman smiled at her. "Deputy Michaels, would you like to read the prisoner his rights before we take him to the station?"

She smiled. "It would be my honor." She walked over and faced Robert. "You have the right to remain silent…"

Brock watched her, and his heart swelled. He knew as she spoke the words her thoughts were on those who had died and those who almost had. Robert Sterling had created havoc on the island, but his reign of terror had been brought to a halt.

As she finished, she turned and caught sight of her sisters standing at the kitchen door. With a cry she ran to them and locked them in a tight embrace. Betsy and Emma sobbed and clung to Kate. Kate tilted her head back and stared upward. Although Brock couldn't hear the whispered words coming from her mouth, he knew she was offering thanks for the survival of her family.

The agents hustled Robert Sterling from the kitchen, but Brock lingered. He stared at the three sisters who didn't appear to notice that he was there. As if she'd read his thoughts, Kate turned to him and smiled. Tears ran down her cheeks. "Thank you for saving us, Brock. If it wasn't for you, we'd be dead."

He shook his head. "I'm sorry I led Robert Sterling here. Doug and all those other people wouldn't be dead if I'd stayed away."

Betsy shook her head and frowned. "You can't think that way. You've saved our family. We're all together again."

A sudden thought struck Brock. "You're not quite all together yet."

The three looked at him. Emma grinned. "What does that mean, Brock?"

He smiled at them. "I received a call from my investigator friend this afternoon. He's coming to Ocracoke tomorrow, and he's bringing your brother, Scott, with him."

Their mouths gaped open. "He's bringing Scott home?" Kate whispered.

He stared into her eyes and hoped that she knew he would have searched forever if it had taken it to find her brother. "Yes."

The three burst into tears and hugged each other again. How he wished they would open their arms and invite him into their circle, but they didn't. After a moment, he turned and walked from the house.

He stopped on the front porch and glanced around. Six years ago he hadn't belonged here, and he had left. During his stay this time he had come to hope that now he could belong, be a part of Kate's family, but it didn't seem likely at this point that his wish would be granted.

Part of his mission had been successful, though. He'd come to Ocracoke to find peace for his battered soul, and he had. Down the beach a Black-crowned Night Heron called. He closed his eyes and smiled. The sweet sound of God's whispers filled his ears.

He glanced up at the sky, which had now darkened into night, and sighed. It was time for him to leave Ocracoke and Kate, and he would. But first, he had to revisit the beach where Kate had first told him to listen for God's voice.

EIGHTEEN

Kate sat on the couch in the living room, Betsy on one side and Emma on the other. Emma snuggled closer and laid her head in Kate's lap. Kate's right arm circled Betsy's shoulders while her left stroked Emma's hair.

"I was so scared," Emma murmured.

Kate's heart was pierced by the fear she heard in Emma's voice. She crooked her finger and looped a wayward strand of Emma's hair behind her ear. "I was, too, Emma."

Emma pushed into a sitting position and stared at Kate. "But you're a police officer. Why would you be scared?"

"Because there are bad people in the world who want to hurt good people, and you're one of the good ones. I didn't want you to be hurt."

Emma smiled. "I prayed that everything would be all right. When I heard Brock's voice, I knew he would save us just like he saved me the night of the fire."

Kate nodded. "Brock was very brave. We owe him a big thanks."

She leaned her head against the sofa back, and Emma did the same. Kate hadn't been able to get Brock's words out of her mind ever since she'd heard him tell Robert how much he loved her. She had expected him to stay and talk with her, but when she'd turned around, he'd disappeared.

Now she didn't know what to think. Maybe he told Robert those things in hopes he might let them go. But he had seemed so serious. Had he really meant it?

"What are you thinking about?" Betsy's voice brought her back to the present.

She opened her eyes and glanced at Emma. "I haven't seen Rascal since he tried to climb up Robert's leg. He may be scared and hiding. Why don't you try to find him?"

Emma grinned and jumped from the couch. "I will."

When Emma had run from the room, Kate turned to Betsy. "I need to talk to you." For the next few minutes she told her sister all that had been said in the kitchen. When she finished, she reached for Betsy's hand. "What do I need to do?"

Betsy clasped Kate's hand in hers. "I can only answer that if I know how you feel. Do you love Brock?"

Kate nodded. "I thought I'd gotten over him, but I haven't. I love him so much, Betsy, but I'm afraid."

"Of what?"

Kate wiped at a tear that escaped her eye. "Brock wants a life in the city. I don't. How can that ever work?"

Betsy smiled. "If you love each other, you'll find a way." She pulled her hand free and gave Kate's shoulder a shove. "Why don't you go find him and talk to him? Maybe things will turn out all right."

Kate took a deep breath and pushed to her feet. "I don't know where he went, but I suppose I should at least go thank him again for saving our lives. Maybe he's at the station with Austin, or he could have gone back to the bed-and-breakfast. I'll go look for him, but I'll have to take our car. My cruiser is still at the corner of Oyster Road and Forest Lane."

She grabbed the keys off the hook on the wall beside the front door and stepped on the porch. She was halfway down the steps before she noticed Brock's car still in the yard.

Hurrying to the driver's side, she peered inside, but he wasn't there.

Kate glanced around the dark yard but didn't see him anywhere. Where could he have gone? The answer came to her, and she smiled. The only place she could think of was the spot on the beach where they'd spent so much time together.

The light from the house lit the path up the dunes as Kate climbed, but the beach beyond resembled an empty void in the dark night. It didn't matter. She knew this beach well, and she knew where she would find him.

The sand shifted under her feet as she moved across the open beach toward the sound of the surf. She squinted in the darkness in an effort to find him. A form materialized in front of her, and she inched forward until she stood beside him.

"Brock," she whispered. "Are you all right?"

The moonlight sparkled on the water and cast a glow across the sand. He glanced up and smiled. "I'm fine. Just sitting out here and listening to God."

She dropped to sit beside him. "What's He saying?"

His arm circled her shoulder, and with a tentative tug he pulled her closer. "He's telling me that I've found what I came here seeking. I've found the peace He wanted to give me all along, and the woman I love told me a few days ago that she had forgiven me for the past." He turned to stare at her. "Have you really forgiven me, Kate?"

She placed her hand on his cheek and moved closer. "You were no more at fault over our breakup than I was. I hope we've both moved beyond that terrible time and forgiven each other."

He caught her hand in his and pressed his lips to her palm. He stared at her. "I love you, Kate Michaels. I've never quit, and I should have tried to work things out between us years ago."

"Maybe it wasn't God's time for us to do that."

He nodded. "I think you're right." He took a deep breath. "Will you marry me, Kate?"

Her breath caught in her throat. Before she answered, they had to climb one more hurdle. "I love you, Brock, and I want to marry you more than I've ever wanted anything, but there's a problem. I'm more tied to Ocracoke now than I was six years ago. I can't leave."

He smiled. "I know, and I don't want you to."

"Then how can we work out that problem?"

He kissed her hand again and stared into her eyes. "I've been thinking. With Doug dead and Calvin off to jail, Hyde County has some job openings for deputies on the island. Do you think Sheriff Baxter might consider hiring me? After all, I'm a certified officer, and I have experience working in law enforcement."

Kate laughed and threw her arms round his neck. "Maybe he will if I put in a good word for you."

Her heart soared as he pulled her closer and lowered his lips to hover above hers. "I love you, Kate. I'm afraid you're stuck with me forever."

"That's the best news I've heard all day." She closed her eyes and thrilled to the touch of his kiss.

The bow of the ferry carrying Scott Michaels slid through the harbor opening toward the dock. Twenty-four hours ago Kate and her sisters had found out that their brother was coming to Ocracoke, and now he was here.

From the parking lot Kate scanned the decks as she clutched Brock's hand. Betsy, Emma and Treasury stood to her left. Their eyes held the same excitement that filled her. Brock turned his head and smiled at her. "It won't be long now. When Don called before they boarded the ferry, I told him we'd be in the parking lot. He'll pull in here as soon as they drive onto the island."

Crew members onboard bustled about as the ship glided into its berth and stopped. Within minutes the ramp had been lowered, and the first cars drove onto the island. With each one Kate stood on tiptoe and strained to see inside. Most of them turned right at the end of the ramp headed into the village instead of left into the parking lot.

After several minutes a black car rolled down the ramp. As the car reached the end of the loading ramp, the left turn signal blinked. Betsy sucked in her breath and turned to smile at Kate. They clasped hands and watched the car pull into the parking lot and come to a stop a few feet away from them.

The driver stepped from the car and waved. "Hey, Gentry. We made it."

Brock waved back. "Glad you're here."

Kate waited, but no one else got out. After a moment, she glanced at Brock. "What do you think is wrong?"

He smiled and released her hand. "Maybe he's worried about seeing three long lost sisters. Maybe you should go to him."

Kate nodded. "Come on, girls. Let's go meet our brother."

Emma, holding a framed picture in her hand, led the way. Before they reached the car, the door opened, and a man stepped onto the pavement. Kate gasped at her first glimpse of her brother. He stood erect, his muscular shoulders straight and his hands to his sides, just as she'd seen her father so many times in her life. His wheat-colored hair tumbled over his forehead, and he brushed it back. Deep-set blue eyes gazed at them. His Adam's apple bobbed as he opened his mouth to speak. "I'm Scott. I'm so happy to be here."

Tears filled Kate's eyes, and she struggled to speak. "I'm Kate."

"Kate." He glanced at Betsy. "Betsy." Then to Emma. "Emma." The names rolled on his tongue as if he was savoring the sweetness of each one.

Emma held out the frame in her hand. "This is for you."

He took it from her, studied the picture and looked up at them. "Who is this?"

The tears spilled from Kate's eyes. "That's our father. We're speechless because you look just like him."

Scott's eyes grew wide, and his trembling hands grasped the frame tighter. "I do, don't I? I've always wondered what my father looked like, and his image was with me all the time."

Betsy nodded. "We're glad you're here. Welcome home, Scott."

Kate didn't know who made the first move, but suddenly the four of them were wrapped in each other's arms. As the tears flowed down Kate's face, she wished her father had lived to see this moment. She'd promised him they would find the son he lost, and now they had.

Three hours later their happiness hadn't subsided as she and Brock sat at the table on Treasury's back porch. In the backyard, Scott, Betsy and Emma sat at a card table in the shade of an oak tree, a game of Chinese checkers in front of them.

The back door of the house opened, and Treasury came out carrying a tray with glasses and a full pitcher of lemonade. She set the tray down on the table where Kate and Brock sat, then sank down into a wicker rocker.

Brock rubbed his stomach. "That was a delicious meal, Treasury."

Before she could answer, Rascal leaped onto the porch and settled at Treasury's feet. She glanced down and smiled. "Well, there's my little darling. I saved you a nice piece of fish for your supper."

Kate and Brock cast surprised glances at each other before they burst out laughing. "I thought you hated Rascal," Kate said.

Treasury shook her head. "Not since he helped save my girls. From now on he's going to be the most pampered cat on this island."

Rascal looked up at her and meowed before he jumped into Treasury's lap and lay down. She patted the cat's head and leaned her head against the back of her chair. Within minutes a soft snore drifted from the chair.

"Hello, everybody!" The greeting echoed in the quiet backyard.

Startled, Kate turned her head to see Grady Teach walking around the side of the house. His hand gripped the handle of a shovel, and the spadelike blade rested on his shoulder. He walked to the back porch, propped one foot on the bottom step and grinned at her and Brock.

Kate smiled. "Where are you going with that shovel?"

Grady pushed his straw hat out of his eyes. "I'm getting ready to go treasure huntin' tomorrow. Anybody want to come help me look for Blackbeard's treasure?"

Kate glanced at Brock, then at her sisters and brother, whose laughter filled the backyard, and at Treasury sleeping with one arm around Rascal. Kate had never been surrounded by so much love.

She reached for Brock's hand, squeezed it and smiled at Grady. "No thanks. I have all the treasure I need right here."

* * * * *

Dear Reader,

Several years ago my son, granddaughter and I took a trip to Ocracoke Island, a small barrier island off the coast of North Carolina. From the moment we drove off the ferry into Ocracoke Village, I was in love with this thirteen-mile-long speck of land twenty-five miles off the mainland. The beautiful beaches, the salt marshes, the island ponies and the wildlife give Ocracoke a unique allure that draws thousands of visitors a year. I knew right away I had to set a book on this island, where Blackbeard the Pirate lived and where he met his death off its coast in 1718.

I have taken some liberties in writing this book, but not with the kindness and love of their island that I encountered from the people who call this place home. I salute the hearty people of Ocracoke and look forward to the time when I can return.

Sandra Robbins

Questions for Discussion

1. Kate struggled with her inability to forgive when some-one had wronged her. Do you have difficulty forgiving others? What did Jesus say about forgiveness?

2. Brock's guilt over an innocent man's death consumed him. Have you ever dealt with guilt because of your actions? How did you cope with your feelings?

3. Kate saw God's presence in the beauty of her island. Do you take time to marvel at the works of God all around you, or do you ignore God's hand in nature?

4. Kate sacrificed her own happiness to take care of her family after her mother's death. Are you willing to put others' needs before your own needs? How have you done that in the past?

5. Kate and Brock encountered deceit and evil in people they trusted. Have you ever had a friend betray you? How did you deal with it?

6. Kate and Betsy knew they would someday be responsible for the aging Treasury. Have you had to take care of an elderly family member? How difficult has it been?

7. Brock realized his selfish attitude was shaped by the fact that he felt abandoned by his father. Have you had to deal with divorced parents? How has it affected your life?

8. Grady devoted most of his time to finding Blackbeard's treasure. Has acquiring money become so important in

your life that you neglect other things? What do you have in your life that money could never replace?

9. When Kate thought she was about to die, she realized how much time she'd wasted by not forgiving Brock. Is there someone you need to forgive?

10. Brock came to realize that God is real and gave his heart to Him. Have you trusted God and turned your life over to him?

INSPIRATIONAL

Inspirational romances to warm your heart & soul.

Love Inspired. SUSPENSE

TITLES AVAILABLE NEXT MONTH

Available August 9, 2011

AGENT UNDERCOVER
Rose Mountain Refuge
Lynette Eason

THE BABY'S BODYGUARD
Emerald Coast 911
Stephanie Newton

BURIED TRUTH
Dana Mentink

ON DEADLY GROUND
Lauren Nichols

LISCNM0711